WRANGLED

STEELE RANCH - BOOK 2

VANESSA VALE

Wrangled

ISBN: 978-1-7959-0005-8

Cover design: Bridger Media

Cover graphic: Deposit Photos- prometeus

GET A FREE BOOK!

JOIN MY MAILING LIST TO BE THE FIRST TO KNOW OF NEW RELEASES, FREE BOOKS, SPECIAL PRICES AND OTHER AUTHOR GIVEAWAYS.

http://freeromanceread.com

1

AMISON

I watched as patrons entered and left the Silky Spur. Being line dancing night at the local bar set at the edge of town, the place was hopping. Unlike everyone else headed in with fun in mind, I fought it. No, I fought myself because *she* was in there. And I was ignoring my dick as it rested down the inside of my thigh, painfully hard and not a chance of going down. If I listened to what that head wanted, I'd be balls deep in her by now. But I didn't live by what my dick wanted—I wasn't nineteen anymore—until now. Until *her*.

I'd seen her go inside with Shamus and Patrick and a few others from the ranch over an hour ago. Yeah, I was stalking her, but she needed someone to watch out for her. To protect her. Compared to some of the women in tiny little shorts that barely covered their ass cheeks and skimpy tops, she was modestly dressed in a jean skirt, cowboy boots and a western shirt.

It didn't matter if she wore that or a burlap sack. I could envision every inch of her body underneath. A petite, voluptuous package. It only mattered that no one else saw all that perfection. I squeezed the steering wheel, knuckles going white, knowing I'd beat the shit out of any guy who laid a finger on her. Except Boone. I wanted to watch him put his hands all over her.

Fuck. I sat out in the parking lot, doing jack-shit. It had been three days since I first laid eyes on Penelope Vandervelk, the second Steele daughter and heiress to arrive in Montana, and since then, I'd thought of nothing but her. Her long blonde hair. How tiny she was. The top of her head sure as shit didn't come up to my shoulder. Her blue eyes. And those tits and ass. For someone so petite, she had more curves than a road through the mountains. No doubt those lush mounds would overflow my palms and her hips...they'd be perfect to grip and hold as I fucked her from behind.

I groaned inside the confines of the truck cab. I wanted her with a desperation I'd never known. I'd seen the way Cord Connolly and Riley Townsend had fallen hard and fast for Kady Parks. While I hadn't laughed at the suddenness, the intensity of their connection, I'd certainly doubted it would ever happen to me. I'd been so fucking wrong. Hell, they'd be laughing at *me* right now if they knew what I was doing. Again, jack shit with a dick as hard as a steel beam.

I wanted Penelope. My dick—and my heart—would have no one else. I didn't see other women now. Too tall, too thin, too...whatever. It didn't matter. They weren't *her*.

The worst part? She was twenty-two. Jesus, I was sixteen years older. *Sixteen!* Enough to know better than to get her all dirty. And what I wanted to do to her would make her filthy. I should leave her the fuck alone. To let her find a boy her own age. Yeah, boy. No kid knew his way around a pussy with any kind of skill. She'd be missing out on what Boone and I could give her, what she deserved. And yet I knew it was wrong. That was why she was in the Silky Spur with Patrick and Shamus. They were still in college, born in the same fucking decade. So were the other ranch hands she was with. They'd invited her to go dancing with them, a group of guys using each other to get closer to her. And yet the thought of one of them touching her—hell, even thinking about getting between those luscious thighs—made me see fucking red.

Boone and I were the ones who would see those pert tits, to suck on her nipples. To taste all that sticky-sweet honey right from the source. To hear her scream our names as she came. As she milked my dick and pulled every drop of cum from my balls.

Fuck, yes. And when she'd drained me dry, I'd watch her take her turn with Boone because one hard dick wouldn't be enough for her. Come morning, she'd not be able to walk properly and she wouldn't remember her own name.

And that was why I was here. I'd held off enough. My dick said go get her. My mind said hands off. Until now. I should have been given a fucking medal for holding off as long as I had. Three days was fucking torture. No more. The very thought of her dancing and wiggling that perfect ass in front of other men toppled the last of my resolve. I'd been waiting for *The One* to come along. Thirty-eight years. This wasn't a one-night stand. This wasn't an itch that needed to be scratched. No. This was the real deal.

I wanted Penelope—forever—and I was going to have her.

Decision made, I grabbed my cell, called Boone.

"I give up."

That was all I said, but he knew exactly what I meant. "'Bout fucking time you got your head out of your ass. My dick is sick and tired of my fist."

It seemed she'd filled both of our fantasies for the past few days. While Boone had blown his load to thoughts of Penelope, I'd held off. I wanted to save up every drop of my cum for her and my balls ached in protest. My fist wasn't going to do any longer. One look at her and I wanted to come with that tight cunt wrapped hot and wet around me. Forever.

Boone had been at the ranch when she'd first arrived, when she'd climbed from her little hatchback loaded with her stuff. Sweet, young, innocent. Fucking gorgeous. He'd given me *the look* and I'd known he'd thought the same as me. She was the one. She was going to be ours. Since I hadn't been ready, had fought like fuck to keep my distance beyond basic introductions, he'd held off approaching her for more. We'd do it together because she would belong to both of us. We'd take her, claim her, fuck her, love her. Together.

Obviously, he'd known I would eventually give in to the blonde-haired temptation. I hated his deep well of patience. I'd hated it ever since we were little kids, the fucker. I didn't go off on a hair trigger, but compared to Boone, I was rash and spontaneous. That's why he made a damn fine doctor. But his words proved he wasn't nearly as laid back about her as I'd thought.

"Come to the Silky Spur," I barked, opening the door to my truck and climbing out. "It's time to claim our girl."

2

 ENNY

I HAD no idea line dancing could be so much fun. I couldn't help the grin on my face or how I felt...good. Now I knew why people said to kick up their heels and have some fun. Fun I'd been missing out on as I'd been head down for months in research and writing my Master's thesis and the outline for my dissertation. Oh, it had paid off; I'd even been emailed an offer to work at an oil and gas company. A few smaller firms had made offers as well, but the international firm was really interested and serious about their offer. But, all the work and the dull—yet highly lucrative—job opportunities only confirmed what I already knew. I didn't want to work in oil and gas. I wasn't living *my* life.

Of course, I'd never been given much of an

opportunity to just have *fun*. My parents—my mother and the man who I'd thought was my father—would have dropped dead if they were seen in a country-western bar. I laughed as I moved my feet in time with the upbeat tempo of the song, learning the steps by following those in the row in front of me. I fumbled, but I didn't care. No one was taking notice of my mistakes, pointing them out and shaming me. No one knew who I was. More importantly, no one knew who my parents were. Thank god.

Everyone stomped and clapped, swayed and turned together. The smoky air was a little steamy from the crowd. Shamus caught my eye as I spun about and gave me a wink and an easy smile. I couldn't help but grin back and wave, then be a beat late in the heel stomp that came next. When the song came to an end, everyone clapped and hollered, some even whistled in that earsplitting way that my parents' housekeeper would use to call in the dogs. I'd never learned the skill, although my mother found the action crass and said that was one of the reasons Mrs. Beauford would never rise above her station.

God, my mother.

Why did I always think of her, of the family, all...the... time? I wasn't at school, nor on my research/work trip in Iceland. I was in Montana and out from under their oppressive thumbs, completely at my mother's disappointment. There was no way they'd come here, even if it were to drag me out of the bar.

No. I was safe from them. Safe wasn't exactly the right word. They weren't *dangerous*. They would never hurt me physically. Emotionally? Yeah, I had some pretty good scars. The only thing I was in danger of with the Vandervelks was losing myself. And Aiden Steele, bless his dead heart, he'd saved me. I wished he was alive so I could thank him, hug and kiss him with an overt and shameful display of public affection. I now knew why I'd never fit in with my family. I took after my father, a father I'd never known existed until two weeks ago. It explained *so* much, even why I possibly liked line dancing. Had he liked it? If he'd worked his way across the country making five illegitimate daughters, then I had to think he'd at least given line dancing a try.

I just had to wonder how a guy like that would have been allowed in my mother's bed for one night. I wiped my brow and licked my parched lips as I worked my way back to the others, trying to wipe the image of my mother having sex with anyone from my mind.

"Having fun?" Patrick asked. He was at a high-top table, his forearms resting on it as he waited for my answer.

"Absolutely." I plucked at my shirt, trying to cool down. The bar was crowded and the dancing made me hot. "Did you get a date?"

He grinned, and even in the dim lighting, I could tell he was blushing. Just after we'd arrived, he'd spotted a woman who he was sweet on—his words, not mine—and had gone over to her.

"Tomorrow night. Ready for a beer?"

I nodded and he poured me a glass from the plastic pitcher in the middle of the table as he told me about her. He was definitely into her. Patrick, Shamus and the other guys were all really nice. And they weren't too bad on the eyes either. No one from Steele Ranch was anything less than handsome. There must be something in the water out here. Or maybe it was the rugged ranch work that tanned their skin and built up their muscles to bulging. But it wasn't any of them whom I thought of. Or their gorgeous physiques. They were fine and all, but more like brothers than guys I'd date...or sleep with. It was Jamison and Boone who melted my butter.

Yes, Jamison *and* Boone.

I'd found the letter from Riley Townsend, the estate lawyer, about my inheritance after my return from Iceland. It had been at the post office with the huge pile of other mail I'd put on hold. For months. Riley had been the one I told of my plans to come to Montana, but hadn't given a definite date or time. I'd driven across the country from North Carolina solo and at that time, had no idea how long it would take. When I finally pulled up to the main house on the ranch, I'd been met by a whole slew of guys. They must have heard me approach or seen the dust kicked up behind my car on the long, dirt driveway. Whatever the reason, my first thought when they walked up was that they were doing a cowboy calendar photo shoot because they were all denim-clad, snap-shirt wearing, Stetson-hatted hotties. One after the other after the other.

But two specifically had caught my eye and stopped my heart. Jamison and Boone. Yes, they were beyond handsome, but the way they looked at me, all steely-eyed intensity as if they could see how nervous I was, how tired, excited, hopeful, they seemed to be able to see *me*.

The others had seemed like young, eager puppies in comparison. Jamison was the Steele Ranch foreman, the man in charge. Boone had said he didn't live on the ranch like the others, was there to check on one of the men recovering from a concussion.

I'd felt small beside them. Being petite, practically everyone over the age of twelve was taller than me, but Jamison had to have an extra foot on me, Boone a little bit more. I should have felt nervous; they could easily overpower or hurt me. I didn't feel that way. No, I felt... protected. And a little stunned because they turned me on. A lot. I *felt* aroused by shaking their hand, being under their close scrutiny. My panties got wet by just a quick introduction, the way their gazes had raked over every inch of me. And I'd thought of nothing but them since. Two older, experienced cowboys who no doubt knew exactly what to do with their hands and...every other *big* part of themselves.

"Sorry Kady couldn't make it," Shamus said, his voice raised over the music. He was an undergrad at the state college studying animal science and would head back for his senior year in a few weeks. "Cord and Riley took her back east. Some kind of going away party. I know she's excited to meet you."

I took a sip of my cold beer, trying to imagine Kady. I knew next to nothing about her, only that she was a teacher and she was in a serious relationship with the lawyer, Riley, and another man. A ménage relationship. I should be surprised, and maybe I was, but only because *I* had the hots for two guys, too. I'd only met them for all of ten minutes, but still. I was...drawn to Jamison and Boone. Crazy? Yes.

I wanted to see them again, to find out if this feeling was a fluke, or more. Jamison didn't seem to hang out with the other guys—since he wasn't here—maybe because he was older, or he didn't like to line dance. I guessed he was closer to forty than thirty. Same with Boone. That didn't bother me, that they were so much older. Nothing I knew—or saw—bothered me one bit.

As for Kady, if she could make a relationship with two guys work and no one seemed to care, perhaps I could as well. God, I was thinking *relationship* and I'd barely had a conversation with either Jamison or Boone. I was being ridiculous. The fact that I hadn't seen them since I'd arrived only proved they most likely didn't even think of me. They'd only been gentlemen in welcoming me. Nothing more.

I took a big gulp of my beer.

"It's fine. She'll be back soon and I'm not going anywhere."

I wasn't. I intended to stay in Barlow. I just had to deal with my mother. Sometime. Just not right now. I was having too much fun. Montana definitely agreed with me.

"Do you have other brothers and sisters?" he asked when there was a lull between songs.

"Besides Kady, I've been told I have three other half-sisters I haven't met. Then I have three steps. One sister and two brothers. All older." They were my father's—no, stepfather's—from a previous marriage and we weren't close, to say the least. Turns out, we weren't even related.

No blood shared between us. Being half-sisters, I hoped Kady and I could at least be friendly.

"It's nice of you to ask me to come along," I said, changing the subject. "Line dancing's fun."

When I asked them what someone wore to such an activity, they'd just looked down at themselves in their jeans and shirts, then told me about the western clothing store in town. Betty, the store owner, had been a big help in finding things that would make me fit in, including the cowboy boots and cute jean skirt.

"Never done it before?" Patrick asked, settling into one of the high stools and grabbing the pitcher to top off his glass.

I shook my head. "Nope. It's not something I did in college and since then, I've been in Iceland." As if that explained it all. It didn't. I'd rushed the same sorority as my mother and line dancing definitely didn't fit that crowd. She wouldn't have liked Iceland either—too wild —but it was where I needed to go to do my research for my degree, so it was *acceptable*. I tried to picture my mother at a country bar and it made me smile. Then thoughts of her getting Aiden Steele in bed returned. Gah. I put my pint glass down, tucked my hair behind my ear. "I'm going to run to the ladies' room. Be right back."

They nodded before I headed off, cutting through the thick crowd to the hallway at the back. I'd have to stop by the store and thank Betty for her help. I blended in perfectly and the boots were fun and completely not me. No, maybe they were the *new* me.

A guy stepped into my way, put his hand on my waist. "Hey there," he said. He was mid-twenties, big. But his smile wasn't kind and his touch was rough. I flinched away, but his fingers dug in.

"Hi," I said, not meeting his eyes. "Headed for the bathroom."

I stepped to my right trying to veer around him. He stuck his arm out, planted his hand on the wall, blocking me.

"I saw you out there dancing. I like your moves." His hot breath fanned over my neck and I cringed.

"Thanks. Look, I have to pee." I quickly ducked under his arm—a perk for being so short—and dashed into the bathroom. Exhaled. I stayed longer than I should, for once thankful for a line, hoping he'd give up or find someone else to chat up. Someone who was interested. I certainly wasn't.

But when I came out, he was still there, leaning against the wall, arms crossed. "Took you long enough."

I frowned, started walking down the hall choosing to just ignore him, but he stepped in my path. "Come on, baby."

"My name's not baby." I veered to the left. He stepped in front of me.

"What is it then? 'Cause I need to know it so I call out the right name when I fuck you."

Gag.

"Not happening." I shook my head, stepped to the right, then the left, trying to get around him. He wasn't the first asshole I'd dealt with and he certainly was persistent. But when he stepped into me, turning us so I back stepped and was pressed against the wall, every hard inch of his body pinning me in place, I began to panic. He smelled of stale beer and BO.

And when his big paw settled on the back of my thigh, I began to fight. It was only a matter of time before it crept upward.

"Let me go." My hands went to his chest to push him off, but he was just too big. Too strong.

"Not until I at least get a little feel."

3

OONE

THE BAR WAS PACKED. I hated crowds, hated loud music. I wouldn't have come through the doors for anything—or anyone—but Penelope. I'd been damned lucky to be out at the Steele Ranch when she'd arrived the other day and all because Davies needed a follow-up visit for his concussion. He was fine, would be back in the saddle within a few days.

As for me? Just the sight of her tight little body made me feel like *I'd* been the one who'd fallen off a horse and whacked his head on a fence post. The damage was done; I'd never be the same again. She wasn't my type; I'd never gone for tiny, curvy blondes, but maybe that was why I was still single. Penelope Vandervelk was one hot, little package and I wanted to unwrap every layer of her until she was bare before me. And Jamison.

I didn't just mean her clothes. Since the other day, I'd checked her out online. Besides being gorgeous, she was smart, too. And that made her even more incredible.

But that didn't mean jack shit if I couldn't get her alone. Jamison had been adamant that we were too old for her. He was right, we were. Hell, going after a twenty-two-year-old when you're thirty-five was close to cradle robbing. She wasn't jailbait, not even barely legal. She had a fucking Master's degree and a few years under her belt to know how things went. How to handle a man with those hourglass curves and hot pussy. My dick found everything about her hot as fuck, even that brilliant mind of hers. I'd left the ranch the other day and had to pull the truck over, take out my dick and rub one out. *On the side of the road.*

I'd fantasized about how her little pussy would feel dripping all over my dick. How it would be hot and wet and eager for my tongue to lap every drop of it all up. And that's when I'd shot like a fucking geyser all over my hand. I hadn't been that horny since I was fifteen.

And Jamison thought we were too old. I'd just had to be fucking patient waiting for Jamison to get his head out of his ass. Fortunately, I'd had two twelve-hour shifts to get my mind out of Penelope's panties. Three days. Three long days of waiting for him to give up the fight. Finally. Fucking finally, he'd let his other head think for him.

I shook my head with impatience as I walked into the bar right behind him. He was immediately hailed by a friend and was forced to say hello. Focusing solely on our gorgeous target, I steered clear and went in search of Penelope, my hard dick practically leading the way.

I spotted the guys from the ranch and pushed through the crowd to their table. A new song came over the hidden speakers and I had to shout to be heard as I looked around. "Where's Penelope?"

Patrick held up a clean pint glass. "Want a beer?"

I shook my head. I didn't want a beer. I wanted my woman. I repeated the question. Patrick leaned in, shouted, "Bathroom."

"Alone?" I countered.

Shamus slapped me on the shoulder. "Since when do we follow a woman to the bathroom?"

I glanced around, took in all the ladies who were scantily dressed, all the men who were checking them out, ready to fuck.

"Since this place is a meat market." I cocked my head in the direction of a woman walking by in a jean skirt the size of a Band-Aid. If she lifted her arms in the air, she'd be ready for a GYN exam. She was beautiful in a fuck-me-now sort of way, but she wasn't Penelope. "You bring a lady to a place like this, you keep a close eye on her. If she goes to the restroom, you wait for her in the damned hallway."

The two boys—they *were* fucking boys—finally looked away from the passing woman's ass and nodded as if I'd imparted some amazing advice.

"She's been gone, like, ten minutes," Shamus said, glancing at his watch.

I knew women and how long it took to do whatever the hell it was they did in the bathroom. But ten minutes?

I saw Jamison approach and I angled my head toward the back. Veering, he caught up to me.

"Leave me alone!"

I heard Penelope's voice before I saw her. That was because this big asshole had her pinned against the wall, blocking almost all of her from view. I couldn't miss the way his meaty paw was sliding up beneath her thigh or the way she was twisting and shifting to avoid it. She lifted her knee to try to make contact with his balls, but she was just too damn small. Instead, she brought her heel down on top of his foot, which made his hand jerk away.

"Let her go, asshole."

He didn't move, only turned his head to look at me. Sneer. He wasn't from around here. Most guys had better manners than this pig and if they didn't, they knew me, knew Jamison and would've walked away by now, his brains—and balls—intact.

"She's a wild one," he replied. Obviously, he had shit for brains.

I heard Jamison's growl a split second before he knocked me to the side and launched himself at the man. The crack of his fist in the asshole's face was loud enough to be heard over the music. So was the heavy thud when he hit the dirty floor. Jamison stood over him, breathing hard, making sure he didn't get back up. A few people skirted around him as they left the bathrooms, but no one said anything.

I went over to Penelope, put my hands on her shoulders and leaned down so we were eye level. Did a quick professional assessment of her. No blood, no marks on her. Her eyes were wide, the pale blue irises only a thin circle.

"Are you okay?"

She nodded, licked her lips. Her breathing was ragged, but she was holding it together. I couldn't miss the thrum of her pulse at the base of her neck.

"I saw his hand on your leg. Did he—"

"No. I'm good. I was about to scream, but you guys, well...you guys took care of him."

I felt a shudder run through her and I pulled her into my arms, hugging her tight. It wasn't for her as much as for me, knowing she was safe and whole, that we'd taken care of her threat. A scream would have worked, and I had no doubt others would have intervened. But seeing the guy have his hands on her...to have him touch what was so perfect, what would be ours—no, what was *already* ours—*fuck* that.

She was all softness and warmth in my hold, her head resting on my chest as I stroked her silky hair. I felt her hands on my lower back, her fingers curled into my shirt and gripping tightly. We watched as two bouncers dragged the guy toward the back door at the end of the hall, Jamison following, hands on hips, to ensure he was put out with the trash.

I leaned down so I could murmur in her ear. While the music was muted here in the hallway, it was still loud. I couldn't resist brushing a kiss against the silky strands. "I'm getting you out of here." She nodded. "Jamison will catch up."

I turned her so my arm was slung around her shoulders, her body pressed right up against mine. No

way was there going to be any space between us. If we
took up too much room, people could just move out of
the fucking way.

"You," I growled, pointing at Patrick, Shamus and
the others with a narrowed gaze. We approached the
table, only slowing down enough to talk. They knew
instantly something had happened, and looked to
Penelope with a mixture of panic and worry. This
was going to be a lesson for them, one they would
never fucking forget. If they didn't protect a woman
in their care, I would make sure Jamison kicked
them off the ranch. If Penelope was going to live
alone in the main house, I had to know she'd
be safe.

After what happened to Kady Parks the month before
with a fucking hit-for-hire, door locks weren't enough in
my mind.

"We'll talk tomorrow."

I didn't wait for them to do more than nod, just cut
through the bar and out to my truck, never releasing my
hold on Penelope. I lifted her up into the passenger seat
—she was so fucking light—and stood inside the open
door, trying not to think of how tiny her waist was
beneath my hands. How I wanted to slide them up and
cup her lush breasts, slide my thumbs over the already
hard nipples. Now wasn't the time.

I took a deep breath, let it out.

"You know I'd never hurt you, right? That you're safe
with me?"

"Safe with both of us," Jamison called as he
approached, his footsteps loud on the asphalt. "You saw

what happens when someone else gets their hands on you."

The parking lot lights cast her in a harsh orange glow, but she'd never looked prettier. Especially since she was sitting in *my* truck, her jean skirt settled halfway up her thighs exposing a few extra inches of her gorgeous legs. I'd wanted her here, alone with both of us, but not because of this reason.

"I know," she replied, her voice soft, steady as she glanced from me to Jamison. "After I met you, I-I looked you guys up online. Know you're good."

Good? Hell, if she knew the things I wanted to do to her, she'd run back inside. Every dirty plan I had that involved her naked, willing body was very, very bad.

Jamison smiled, which was a rare sight. "What did you find, Kitten?"

I expected his voice to be harsh with anger, the adrenaline hard to burn off, but he sounded almost... tender. Especially with the endearment that suited her perfectly. I was used to it from working in the ER and was acclimated to the quick burn of energy. At least he got to punch the fucker. That must have felt damned good.

"I know you run the ranch and that you used to be a police officer in Denver. And Boone, you're a doctor."

"None of that ensures we're the good guys," I told her. But I didn't mention I'd done some research on her as well. I had no idea how she'd made it out in the world all fragile and tiny as she was. She could be hurt so easily and that fucker who was sprawled by the dumpster was the perfect example. I doubted he was the first, but he definitely was the last to fuck with her.

Instead of climbing out of my truck in fear, she rolled her eyes and smiled. "I understand all too well. Someone's resume doesn't ensure they're not jerks. But I've got a good sense about you two. I just...feel, know you're good."

I didn't know what to say to that, so I glanced at Jamison.

"We're not taking you home now. Not after that," he said, putting his hand up on the truck cab, leaning in. "Let's get some coffee. Let things settle first."

Damn straight. The guy had been aggressive, and if she was going to break down, she wasn't doing it alone.

She glanced between us, offered us a small smile. "All right."

She might have been comfortable with us, but we were sure fucked. She'd slipped right past an attraction and become an obsession. With something bad almost happening to her, it only proved how much she meant to me. And that was fucking insane since I'd known her all of fifteen minutes.

Yup, *fucked.*

4

ENNY

"WE CAN KILL HIM, you know. Just let us know and no one will find the body," Jamison said.

We were sitting at a hard-laminate booth in the gas station at the intersection with the county road that led to the main highway. While I didn't think either of these men brought dates to the Quik-n-Lube, with the scent of hot dogs kept warm all day on metal rollers and the store's fluorescent glow as poor mood lighting, it was the only other place open at this time of night. Besides the Silky Spur. I sat on one side, facing the wall of refrigerated beverages and the hallway to the bathroom. Boone was across from me, his knees bumping into mine beneath the table. I tried not to think about the innocent touch, but it was impossible. Boone was big and gorgeous and hot and just the touch of his knees had me flustered.

Where Jamison was all rugged cowboy, Boone was all broody with his dark looks and quiet intensity. Black hair that was a little too long, piercing eyes, strong jaw...strong everything. He wasn't darkly tanned like Jamison, but being a doctor obviously kept him indoors more. From what I'd read of him, his quiet and watchful demeanor hid his intelligence. They might think I've got some diplomas on the wall, but Boone had a few more than me.

He was a watcher. I recognized the signs, because I was one, too. Jamison seemed to assess a situation and when needed, didn't hold back. Like with the guy at the bar. He punched first, asked questions...never.

Jamison had dropped off two coffees for us and returned with his. He placed it on the faux wood surface, grabbed a metal chair with a vinyl cushion, turned it to face backwards and sat down, his forearms on the high back.

"What?" I asked, my mouth falling open.

"We'll kill the guy who touched you. Steele Ranch has thousands of acres to bury him," Jamison repeated. His tone and the serious look in his eye made me realize he wasn't joking. A guy had touched me and he'd not only knocked him unconscious, but would kill him if I wished it. "I'd make Patrick, Shamus and the others do the hard work of digging the hole, nice and deep, just because they didn't protect you."

Boone's look said he was in complete agreement, but probably couldn't voice the words since he'd taken an oath as a doctor to do no harm. No, that wasn't it. He'd back his friend in a heartbeat.

These two...they were intense. Fiercely protective. A thrill shot through me because that intensity, that fierce protectiveness, was directed all at me. It was potent.

"That...um, won't be necessary." They stared at me intently—Jamison's gaze a piercing gray, Boone's almost black. "I'm fine. Really. And it's not their fault."

Jamison leaned forward more. "Kitten, it is their fault. They take you out, they keep you safe. Period."

I wasn't going to argue with him about it because nothing I said would sway his opinion. My mind got stalled on the way he called me Kitten. I liked it. A lot. I cleared my throat. "Thank you for coming to my rescue."

I *was* thankful. I'd spurned unwanted advances before on my own, many times, but it felt really good having someone step in and help. I'd just never expected it to be these two. I hadn't even known they were at the bar, much less keeping an eye on me. God, watching them in action had been exhilarating. The testosterone in the hallway had been so great I could practically breathe it in. It had been elemental. Like two cavemen staking a claim and fighting for what was theirs.

Slightly unrealistic, because I *wasn't* theirs. They'd just been gentlemen. Protecting me. I had no doubt if Patrick or the others had found me first, they'd have clocked the guy, too. I doubted, though, that any of the others would make me feel eager for them to drag me by the hair back to their cave after. Oh yes, and then they'd have their way with me, doing whatever it was to continue to show their dominance. Not that I had any idea what that was first-hand, but I had a good idea.

I'd seen movies. Even some porn. Being a virgin didn't mean I was clueless. Although…I'd thought that had been true up until now. With Jamison and Boone, I had a feeling what I *thought* happened between a man and a woman was simply Tab A in Slot B. They seemed like guys who would be *very* thorough and didn't stick to the basics. No doubt they were experienced. Ridiculously so. I glanced at their hands wrapped around their disposable coffee cups. Big with long fingers, veined. Strong. I shifted in my seat because my pussy throbbed. Even their hands were hot.

"You don't have to thank us for keeping you safe," Boone said. He spun his cup around on the smooth surface. "Tell us about you."

I shifted, the backs of my thighs sticking to the hard bench. "What do you want to know?"

"Everything," they said at the exact same time.

My eyebrows went up.

Boone leaned forward, put his forearms on the table. Fixed his dark stare on mine. Didn't even blink. I swallowed, licked my lips and he watched that action closely.

"Well, I'm from North Carolina. I just finished graduate school."

"You're pretty young for that," Jamison said, then took a sip of his coffee. Winced and put it down.

"Twenty-two," I countered. "I skipped third grade."

"Was it just you and your mother growing up?" Jamison asked.

I shook my head, tucked my hair behind my ear. "My mother married my stepfather when she was pregnant with me. That was what I'd just learned. I *thought* the ring had come first, that Peter Vandervelk was actually my father, but that wasn't the case."

I flicked my gaze from my cup to the guys. They were watching me closely, but remained quiet. Waited for me to say more.

"He has three older kids from a previous marriage. Two are doctors now, the other a lawyer."

"Impressive," Jamison replied neutrally.

I thought of Kyle, Ryan and Evelyn. Their drive *was* impressive. A neurosurgeon, a thoracic specialist and the youngest female partner ever in her Charlotte law firm. I shrugged because while they were brilliant in their fields, they weren't very nice people.

"Any chance your mother is Congresswoman Vandervelk?" Boone asked.

The corner of my mouth tipped up. "You looked me up, just as I did for you."

He nodded. I was actually kind of glad they already knew some things about me because I didn't have to go into detail. I didn't have to tell them that my mother had lied, not only to me but the entire world, about who my father was. How it was more important for her to keep up with appearances with her constituents than for me, her own daughter, to know the truth.

"Why do you want to hear what you already know?" I wondered aloud. I put my hands in my lap, wiping my sweaty palms on my skirt.

"Because I want to hear it from you," Boone replied simply.

I sighed. "Yes, my mother is a member of Congress. My stepfather is the Vice Chancellor of a university hospital in Charlotte. Fancy titles for fancy people."

"You studied science," Boone added.

I was surprised he wasn't asking more about my parents. That was what most people did. They either wanted something from them or at least the connection to them through me.

"Yes, my focus was subsurface geoscience."

They both listened intently, their eyes squarely on me as if I was the only thing around, the only thing of interest, not the guy who was asking the cashier for directions or the beeps for the gas pumps.

"I spent months in Iceland finishing my thesis, which I won't bore you with. That's why I didn't know about the inheritance or Aiden Steele. Any of it, until I came back. My mail had been on hold."

"I had to do tons of science for med school, but I have no idea what subsurface geoscience is." Boone was being open. Honest. They both were. And they were actually interested in me. In my life. No networking to get to my parents.

"Subsurface geoscience? In three words: Oil and gas."

Jamison rubbed a hand over the back of his neck. I couldn't miss the ruffling of his short hair, a contrast to the tanned skin. I wondered if it was soft to the touch, if his skin was warm, what it would feel like against my lips. I was thinking all these hot, distracted thoughts about them. Had been from the first time I saw them. I'd never really considered a guy enticing enough to have sex with. Before now. Sure, I'd met handsome men, but none of them had *done it* for me. Now, all of a sudden, my hibernating libido decided to wake up. Like a toddler after eating too much sugar, wired and raring to go. I wanted Jamison. I wanted Boone, and I wasn't exactly sure what to do about it. I had no idea how to seduce one man, let alone two.

"There are good careers in that, especially around here."

Yes, in this part of the country, mineral rights, oil and gas rights, extraction even, were big news. A big deal. There were many issues between environmentalists and extraction companies. Big money. Big destruction, too. Crazy things like increased radon levels and even man-made earthquakes. It was a political nightmare.

"Yes, I've been wooed already. Job offers." I gave them a quick, small smile. "But I've got my dissertation outline for my PhD that comes next."

"You don't sound very excited about that. The jobs or the PhD," Jamison murmured, studying me closely, as if he could hear the truth past the words.

A customer came inside and the bell above the door dinged. He went to the counter, asked for a pack of cigarettes.

"A Vandervelk is high achieving." The words were like a mantra, drilled into me since birth. I replied automatically and without even thinking.

"What the hell does that mean?"

I flicked my gaze up to Boone and he was frowning. He looked mad.

"I'm Penelope Vandervelk." I tapped my finger on my chest. "I'm expected to maintain a certain level of accomplishment. I mean, it wouldn't look good for my mother, or any of the others, if I—"

Both men leaned forward so they were close, a little too close. "If you what?"

"If I did what I wanted," I admitted.

"What do you want to do, join the circus?"

I smiled, the idea ridiculous, yet it would be so much fun to tell my mother that. "Of course not."

"Did you *want* to study about oil and gas?"

I shook my head. I couldn't believe the way they were digging deep, getting past all the fake smiles and stories I had in place for, well, everyone. I'd learned from the expert on how to converse without really saying anything important. But Boone and Jamison? I couldn't give false answers. If they could read me so well, could *see* me so well, they'd see my lies, too. I didn't want to be fake with them. Didn't want to have lies between us. I *wanted* them to know the truth. The real me.

"You spent years studying a major you didn't want," Jamison said. "And you're planning to continue on, get your PhD just so...what? Your mother can keep up appearances?"

I fiddled with my coffee cup and Jamison took it from me, put his hand on top of mine. I glanced at it, so big, mine was lost beneath. Hard tabletop against my palm, a warm, yet calloused hand gently offering reassurance above.

"I didn't have a choice," I admitted.

"Why not?"

I licked my lips, met Jamison's eyes. "Because they would have cut me off."

Boone leaned back in the booth, laughed and slowly shook his head. "You don't need their money, sweetheart." The term of endearment was laced with sarcasm and immediately put me on edge. There wasn't any warmth to it like when they called me Kitten. "With your degree, you should do just fine on your own. Like you said, you've had job offers. You won't starve, although you might not get the Jag right away."

I jerked my hand out from under Jamison's and slid across the booth, stood. I suddenly felt cold and very alone. "We're done here."

5

ENNY

JAMISON'S ARM hooked about my waist before I took a step, pulled me back so I was tucked into his side. With him sitting, his eyes were right in line with my breasts. His arm was strong, yet his hold was relaxed.

"Easy, Kitten. Tell us what's got your claws out."

I narrowed my eyes at Boone, angry that he'd jumped to assumptions. Especially since he was just like all the others, thinking I was spoiled. Coddled. Given everything I could ever want. How little they knew.

"Yes, my family is rich," I told them, my voice tart. But, I kept it low. Not that the guy behind the counter cared if I shouted or not. With the number of customers coming in and out, any kind of outburst would probably be excitement for him. "It paid for seven years of boarding school. Ivy League college. I didn't ask for any of it. I don't care about the money. If I don't do what's *expected*, they'll cut me off. Entirely."

Jamison stood, spun his chair about, sat back down and pulled me onto his lap between one heartbeat and the next. His tug had been gentle, yet he'd moved me so easily, reminding me of the differences in our size, our strengths. He maneuvered me right where he wanted me, and that was tucked in close. My hands went to his shoulders for balance at the surprise shift, although his arm was still banded about my waist. I couldn't miss the hard expanse of his thighs beneath me, the heat of his body or his clean scent. Not cologne, something subtler, like soap and rugged man. "Jamison!" I cried, trying to get up, to at least shimmy my jean skirt back down a little, but he only tightened his hold, securing me in place.

I felt tiny in his lap, my head tucked beneath his chin, my feet nowhere near the linoleum floor.

Boone reached out, tipped up my chin, his dark eyes meeting mine, pinning me in place. The heated stare made me forget all about being in Jamison's lap. "I didn't mean to hurt you with my words. But sometimes pulling out a splinter requires a little pain. You mean they'd cut you from the family."

I nodded. Admitting it *was* painful, and the truth had been festering. It wasn't as if I ever really had their love to begin with, but I'd hoped. Always hoped that I'd get some scraps of affection from them, even from seven states away at boarding school or another country doing my thesis.

"That's why—" I cleared my throat, forced the tears

away. I had no idea why it always upset me, perhaps because while my family wasn't anything like the one I wanted—one where there was no question as to the love that was shared, the laughter, the connection—it was the only one I had. "That's why the inheritance from Aiden Steele, from my...father was perfect timing. I'd finished my Masters and am not eager to continue to get my doctorate. I learned the truth, confronted my mother. She couldn't deny it, not with the legal documents Riley sent. Even my sister, the lawyer, was impressed. I always wondered why I wasn't like them. So focused. Driven to be the best."

"To get a Masters by twenty-two in that specialized field is driven," Jamison pointed out.

"I'm also indifferent, which is a waste. I could handle the study load, but I didn't really care about it. I didn't feel passionate about what I was doing. And that's why I just never fit in. Why my mother was always cool toward me, why the others never liked me. Now I have the answer. I was never really part of the family."

"I'm surprised you didn't know."

I shook my head and Boone dropped his hand. "My mother is a politician. You think having a baby out of wedlock, even years before she took office, is good for her image? My mother and father—stepfather—aren't the close, loving couple. They don't even live in the same state most of the year. I have no idea why they married. Well, I know why my *mother* married. She was pregnant with me. She wasn't in politics then, but still, she had the mindset. Of course, her affair, fling, whatever it was, with Aiden Steele, was a secret. Still is. At least until now, until he died and made me heir. That's why I'm in Montana on *vacation*."

Boone's gaze narrowed as I spoke and I saw the tension building in him. "Vacation?"

"Mmm hmm, a quiet place where I can get my dissertation outline pulled together for my advisor and the review board. That's what we agreed on. That I'd take this time to figure out the inheritance without giving away the truth. And get the outline done, of course."

"What are you really going to do?" Boone asked, cocking his head to the side.

I studied the way his white t-shirt stretched so perfectly over his broad shoulders, the muscles beneath so well-defined. I itched to reach out, run my fingertips over them, feel their power. Instead, I shrugged. "It's a relief actually," I said, not answering his question. "To know the truth, to finally understand. Now I can go after what I want." I flicked my gaze up to Boone's. "The only thing I've ever wanted."

"What's that?" Jamison asked, his turn to prod. His hand slid up and down my back, slow and gentle. It was warm. A soft caress. Soothing. It seemed he was very good at lulling the words from me.

"A family of my own. I know I'm young, too young to think this way, but that's what I want." I didn't hesitate this time, didn't falter because this was what I'd dreamed of for so long. For as long as I could remember. Lying in bed at night at boarding school, wishing I had a family that wanted me around. I wanted my own home. The scent of cooking coming from the kitchen. A husband who would see only me, want only me. Share a bed, love.

To give me the herd of children I wanted who would make a huge mess of the house and bring chaos and insanity. Stained carpet. Dirty dishes in the sink. Muddy shoes on the wood floors. Everything that had been forbidden for me growing up.

But no guy I'd ever met wanted to hear about getting serious right away. Date for a while, maybe move in together for a few years. Possibly. But they were all thinking short term. Really short term, like one night. That was why I never told anyone the truth, never really dated. Why I was still a virgin.

I didn't want to rule the world; I wanted to be Suzy Homemaker. I wanted babies. I wanted a family, a house, a dog. All of it. Aiden Steele had given me the opportunity to get it. A nest egg—a very large one—a house and the chance to be me. The real me. I'd lose my family, but I'd just discovered they really hadn't *been* my family. And that was pure relief. If they shut me out, then I knew now it was because I hadn't belonged anyway. I couldn't be kicked out of a family where I'd never actually belonged.

The trouble behind my dream was finding the man. A man who'd want a relationship. I wasn't the kind of woman who would settle for less. I didn't do casual. Patrick and Shamus were way too young. They'd want the sex, absolutely, to punch my V-card, but not the results. Orgasms, yes. Long term? No.

And as for Jamison and Boone? I was attracted to them, wanted them. I told them the truth. They knew it now. Knew of the relationship bombshell and I knew they'd bolt. I bit my lip, waited. No doubt I'd be back at the ranch, alone, within the hour, neither man to be seen again.

I'd never wanted a one-night stand. I'd had opportunities, but I'd turned every one of them down. I wanted it all and if these two didn't want to give it to me, then I wasn't any worse off than before. I'd survive. I barely knew them. I could become better acquainted with my vibrator and be patient for the right guy to come along. I wasn't going to compromise. I'd done so my whole life with the Vandervelks. I'd done what they'd wanted. Demanded.

No longer. My ovaries were running the show now. And they were popping out eggs for Jamison and Boone.

Boone growled, then turned sideways so he sat facing out of the booth. He crooked his finger and Jamison nudged me off his lap so I stood between Boone's parted knees. Seated as he was, I was taller than him, and it seemed strange to look down at one so big. I frowned. Confused at what he wanted.

"Should I call a cab?" I asked, not sure if they even had any out here.

"Cab?" he asked. Boone snared me with his gaze and I felt Jamison at my side. They were close. Closer than two men should be.

I nodded. "Don't worry. I wasn't going to trap you or anything. You just pulled the truth out of me. I don't mean anything by it, didn't mean *you* specifically. I'll find the right man eventually."

Boone's big hand cupped my jaw and I was thinking about the feel of the callouses on his palm when his lips met mine. I gasped at the soft feel; the brushing of his mouth was remarkably gentle, as if sampling. Learning. He took that opportunity and his tongue delved and found mine. I gasped again at the pulse of heat I felt at the bold caress. The wet heat was shocking, exhilarating. I'd been kissed before. I might have been a virgin, but I spent my teens in boarding school and college. I'd just been a little too young to do more than that.

I settled my hands on Boone's shoulders, felt the play of his muscles as he kept kissing me, using his palm to angle my head as he wanted. His fingers tangled into my hair and I felt his own need in that and in the intensity of the kiss.

I was warm all over, languid. My nipples hardened against the cotton of my bra and if Boone ever lifted his head, he'd see the evidence of my response. What he wouldn't be able to see was that my panties were ruined.

Boone pulled back and I realized I'd closed my eyes. I blinked them open.

"What was that for?" I asked, my voice breathless. Quiet.

Boone's pupils were almost black now, his gaze focused squarely on my lips. His were wet. Reddened. He was affected, too.

"I've been wanting to do that since the second I laid eyes on you. Fuck, you taste good," he said as an afterthought, more to himself, as he licked his lips.

"I thought you didn't even like me," I countered, confused. Or my brain was mush from this kiss. Or both.

"Why would you think that?" His breath fanned over the line of my jaw as he kissed, nibbled and licked his way to my ear.

I tilted my head to give him better access, the slide of his teeth making goosebumps rise on my bare arms.

"Besides your bold questioning? Because the other day you said, 'Nice to meet you' and walked away."

He grunted, nipped my earlobe. "That's because the fucker beside you wasn't ready to claim you yet."

When had Jamison put a hand on my back? It had to be his because Boone's were tangled in my hair and on my hip. The perk of being with two men—extra hands.

"Penelope," Jamison began.

"Penny," I countered, trying to catch my breath still. And my wits. Boone was making me very, very distracted. Or it was the pheromones pumping from him? Or the taste of him on my lips? "Only my family calls me Penelope."

"Penny's good, but I like Kitten better," Jamison replied.

Boone pulled his fingers from my hair so I could turn my head and look at Jamison.

"I thought we were too old for you," Jamison admitted.

My aroused gaze roved over his face. Took in the little wrinkles around his eyes, the creases in his cheeks. He was thirty-eight, not sixty. I didn't see *old*. I saw wise. Experienced. Rugged. Hot. Appealing. I stared at his mouth. Just as kissable as Boone. I wanted to know what he tasted like, too.

"And now?" I asked. Nervous. If he didn't want me, that was fine. I'd had crushes before. It was survivable. Or Boone wanted me and Jamison didn't. Boone *was* a few years younger, or so I thought. But I didn't want just

Boone. Somehow, for some strange, insane reason, I wanted both of them. And without Jamison, something would feel missing.

I watched as the fist on his thigh unclenched.

"And now, I don't give a shit. Now that we know what you want, that we want the same exact thing, we can give it to you."

He stood and I angled my head up to keep my eyes on his. He held out his hand.

"Time to go. It's my turn to kiss you, and I don't want an audience."

 AMISON

I WANT a family of my own.

Kitten's words—oh yes, she was Kitten now—made me instantly hard. No, I'd been hard for three fucking days. It made my dick throb against my thigh and my balls ache. The thought of getting between those creamy thighs and filling her with my cum had me ready to come like an overeager teenager.

She wanted exactly what I wanted. A family, a spouse, a baby. No, lots of babies. I wanted them with her, but that was why I'd stayed away. Because what twenty-two-year-old wanted to be tied down, to have a baby? Turned out, Penelope Vandervelk. My Kitten.

When I was twenty-two, it was the last thing on my

mind. I'd finished college and joined the police academy. Boone had yet to finish college and start med school. Neither of us had been in a place to even think about settling down. The fact that Penny wanted exactly what we wanted to give her made it seem like fate. Was it even possible? Could we be so lucky?

I understood her need, the desperation to belong, to be loved. The shit she'd said about her family made me want to punch more than just a handsy asshole. Who the fuck sent their kid to boarding school for seven years? A parent who didn't want that kid around. No wonder she wanted to make a family of her own. Hers had been shit. She wanted one who would love her unconditionally. Wanted a husband and kids she could love in ways she never received.

Tonight, we'd show her how it could be with us. How we'd get her between us and cherish her with every touch of our hands, every deep thrust of our cocks. She'd come so many times she'd forget everything but our names.

In the back seat of Boone's truck, she was in my arms and my mouth was on hers. I'd waited until he started to drive before I pulled her close—as close as the seatbelts would allow—and tasted her for myself. Watching Boone kiss her had been hot as fuck, but I'd wanted my turn. I had it now. Boone drove while I learned the curve of her lips, the feel of her tongue as it tangled with mine, the way her breath caught when I nipped at the plump bottom lip, heard her moan when I licked the delicate swirl of her ear.

"Where are we going?" she breathed, her chin tilted up as I licked a line down her neck.

It was a cool night, but inside the truck, things were hot and heavy.

"We're going to Boone's. His bed's the closest," I breathed. I couldn't lift my lips from her skin. Had to feel the silky heat of it. Taste the sweetness, breathe it in. "You're going to take our cocks for a wild ride."

"Oh," she said, more as a surprise as my hand cupped her breast than in response to my words.

She was a lush handful, the nipple hard as my thumb brushed over it through her shirt and bra. Her body shifted against me. Damn, she was responsive. Hot. Passionate, and we still had our clothes on. I could only imagine what she'd be like once I got inside her. We were like teenagers making out in the back of a car, although this time, sinking inside her was a given. And I was old enough to want a soft mattress.

Fuck, this wasn't a slow burn. It was scorching hot— had been from the very first—and there was no way she could miss the thick feel of my dick. Nothing was going to hide it; it had yet to go down. After being in a state like this for three days, I had to wonder if it ever would again with Kitten nearby. Hell, I just had to think about her and I was hard.

"Did you think he was talking about horseback riding, Kitten?" Boone asked from the front seat. I turned my head slightly, caught his eye in the rearview mirror, although his dropped to my hand on her tit. I recognized the look. He wanted her. Wanted this.

Every time she breathed, she filled my palm. "I've never ridden before," she said.

I smiled against her ear, kissed it. I loved that we

made her thoughts scatter to say something so odd. "Don't worry, tomorrow we'll go to the ranch and you'll get a nice gentle mare."

I moved back to her mouth. Devoured it.

"That's. Not. What. I'm. Talking. About," she gasped each word between kisses.

The truck veered to the shoulder and Boone slammed on the brakes, both Kitten and I jerking against our seatbelts. He shifted to look back at us.

"What the fuck, Boone?" I asked, glancing at Kitten to make sure she was okay.

He ignored me, his eyes roving over her from her swollen, wet lips to where my hand was cupping her breast, to the expanse of thigh exposed. "That's not what she's saying."

Maybe it was because I'd just had my tongue in her mouth or maybe it was because I did have a glorious handful of her killer curves, but my brain wasn't working as well as it should.

Pulling back, I looked into Kitten's glazed eyes. It was dark, but I could see by the green lighting from the dashboard that she was half-gone with her need.

"Is it?" Boone added.

She shook her head, her tongue flicking out to lick bottom lip. The scent of strawberries swirled around me. Shampoo? Her mouth was that sweet and I knew her pussy would be as well. Warm and sticky, too.

"She doesn't give a shit about a horse," Boone said. "She's never ridden a *man* before. A nice big, hard dick. That pussy's untried."

I dropped my hand in stunned surprise and she whimpered. "You're a virgin?"

I watched her swallow, nod. "Yes."

I closed my eyes, blocked the gorgeous sight of her out. I was too close to coming as it was. Knowing we were the ones to take her cherry, to stretch out that virgin pussy to make it fit just our cocks made my cock throb. I groaned.

"I'm sorry. I didn't think it was a bad thing," she whispered. "Maybe this is happening too fast."

"Fuck no," Boone said, with his usual tact. "We just have to go about this a little different. We'll take you tonight, but we'll have to go gentle. Slow. Even though I'm a doctor, I'm pretty sure a woman needs an easy time of it after getting her cherry popped."

I opened my eyes, looked at my friend, gritted my teeth and nodded. Yeah, we were going to do this different. Slow, even if it fucking killed me.

PENNY

"MAYBE THIS ISN'T such a good idea," I said, my steps slowing as Jamison held my hand and led me into the house.

Boone had parked his huge pickup truck in a three-car garage. While it was the only vehicle in the large space, he also had a three-wheeler ATV, a dirt bike and a pop-up camper. All were spotless, not a fleck of mud or wilderness on them. As was the rest of the garage. It seemed Boone, the neat-nick, liked the outdoors in his off time.

Boone pushed the button to close the overhead garage door, then turned. "We're not like that asshole at the bar. We won't make you do anything you don't want. We're not going anywhere. We've got forever to get to know each other."

"That's just it," I countered, tugging my hand from Jamison's hold and crossing my arms. Not to be defiant, but to keep from reaching out again. I liked touching them. I liked the feel of Jamison's hand in mine and on my breast and I *wanted* it other places. I barely trusted myself around them because they made me feel things I never had before. I'd been into a guy. Hot for him. Or so I'd thought. That had been a tepid bath in comparison. My skin was sensitive, my nipples were hard and ached to be touched. My pussy...god, the inner walls of my pussy clenched in eager anticipation of their big cocks. For the first time ever, I wanted it. No, *needed* it as if my survival were dependent upon it.

Yeah, we had to talk first because I was about to jump them. Climb them like a tree and hope they gave me wild monkey sex.

"Let's take this inside," Boone said, opening the interior door, waited for me to proceed him into the house. He put a hand on my waist to guide me in the dark and flicked on lights to a great room. A stone fireplace rose two stories beside a wall of windows. I could only imagine what the view was beyond. Now, all I could see was inky blackness. With the soft lamps lit on either side of a large sectional sofa, I envisioned curling up here on a cold winter's night by a roaring fire and reading. The space was masculine. Dark wood floors and trim, crisp white walls. An open kitchen was connected. Knotty pine cabinets, thick granite and plenty of stainless steel appliances. Either he didn't cook or he cleaned up after himself because everything sparkled. The house was well and simply decorated.

"It's not the sex," I said, glancing between them. Jamison leaned against the wall, observing. As if he didn't want to get any closer to me, as if he needed a dozen feet to restrain himself. I couldn't miss the thick outline of his cock. It didn't tent his jeans like I'd seen in movies that spoofed the male condition. No, it was like a thick pipe down the inside of his thigh.

That was going to fit inside me? My pussy throbbed with eagerness to find out.

Boone dropped onto the couch and held out his hand to indicate I should sit, too.

I lowered myself a little more daintily, made sure my jean skirt didn't ride up. I was all flustered and horny from their kisses, from Jamison's bold touches in the truck. They couldn't miss the way my nipples poked against my shirt, even through my bra. There was nothing I could do about my traitorous body. It knew what it wanted. *Them.*

I was considered very smart, but perhaps in this, I was being an idiot. Women everywhere would kill for a chance to be with two gorgeous cowboys, cowboys who'd kissed the daylights out of me, and I was *talking*. It just proved they were gentlemen. At least for now. I had a feeling once we were all naked, they'd behave anything but. And that was what my pussy was hoping.

Boone only arched one dark brow, so I licked my lips again and continued.

"You're all ready to say forever with me. We've just met. It's...too soon. Too fast."

Jamison pushed off the wall, came around to sit on the large wooden coffee table before me. He put his hands on my knees, but did nothing more. His skin was warm and the simple touch shot little currents of pleasure...everywhere. "Do you just want a wild night of fucking? Is that what you need?"

His tone was as rough as the words.

I shook my head, my hair sliding over my shoulder. I tucked it back behind my ears. "No. If I did, I could have slept with Patrick or the others. Or any guy at college."

I tacked the last on because I saw the way their gazes narrowed, their jaws clenched at the mention of Patrick touching me.

"Then you want us to fuck you?" Boone asked.

I blushed. I could feel the heat in my cheeks. Just the thought of doing more with them than kissing, or them kissing me in *other* places made me shift in the comfortable seat. "Yes."

"So you want a one-night stand with us specifically," he added.

I shook my head. "Yes. I mean...no." I closed my eyes, took a deep breath. Confused. Flustered.

"What do you want?" Jamison asked, his thumbs moving in circles on the insides of my knees, parting them slightly.

It was mesmerizing. Soothing. Completely distracting. My eyes fell closed and I just felt.

"I want more than that. More than sex."

"But you barely know us. We've just met," he countered. His voice was low, even. Soothing.

"It doesn't matter," I replied, my eyes opening to meet his gray gaze. I felt the insane pull between us. The electrical charge in the air, the need. "I can't explain it, but I just know that I want you, that I want it all."

Neither said anything, instead grinned broadly. Blinded me with their good looks. I'd thought they'd been panty dropping with their brooding gazes, but this? I had no defenses strong enough for wicked smiles.

"Well?" I asked, frowning. Waiting.

"Think, Kitten," Jamison prodded. "Use that gorgeous brain of yours."

I thought about everything we'd just said and realized they'd talked me in a full circle. My whole concern was that they'd been interested in me too quickly, when I had fallen for them just as fast. They'd gotten me to admit as much. I wanted them just as voraciously as they wanted me, even if we'd just met. Time didn't matter, just like Jamison's concern about age difference. It didn't change a thing. Nothing mattered but being with them.

"Oh." I *was* an idiot.

"Oh," Boone replied, sliding across the couch to get closer, to use his fingers to brush my hair back over my shoulder, lean in and kiss my neck.

I whimpered, the need that had been simmering instantly flared back to life.

"So my talk of wanting a family didn't scare you off? I

don't do casual. I'm not wired that way," I whispered, tilting my head to the side.

I felt Boone's lips turn up in a smile against my neck, just before he flicked his tongue out and licked a spot I had no idea was so sensitive.

"We're here, aren't we?" Jamison asked, his hands sliding up the insides of my thighs. His fingers were a few inches shy of my panties.

"Do you want both of us? Two men. Not just one night. Not for a wild ride. For more," Boone said.

I nodded and Boone's hand cupped the back of my head, turned me so he could kiss me. There was no gentleness now. His mouth opened over mine, his tongue demanding immediate entrance. I couldn't deny him. I didn't want to.

"Say it, Kitten," Jamison said, pulling his hands away. "Because we won't fuck you and take your virginity unless you do. This is so much more than one night."

I opened my eyes, looked at him, squirmed as Boone nibbled at the base of my neck. His cheeks were flushed, his lips clamped into a thin line. He was tightly leashed and I knew all that need, that dominance he was holding back, was just for me.

"God, this is crazy, but yes, I want you both. For more than one night. For...everything."

I did. I wanted it all. The hope these two instilled in me, along with the lust, was heady. I should run the other way. Men only wanted in your pants for a night, that was all. I knew guys would say anything to get sex. Promise things then yank them away the following morning. To walk away. But I knew, deep down, Jamison and Boone weren't like that.

Technically, I was Jamison's boss. Kady, too. He'd be giving up a lot for an easy lay. There had been so many sexy, eager women at the Silky Spur who'd be satisfied by a quick romp and nothing more. Barlow was a small town. If it turned out Boone just wanted a fling, he wouldn't be able to hide from me. I was confident he had no intention of moving away, not being a local doctor. They wanted this as much as me. They *felt* the connection.

"Then it's time to break in that pussy, Kitten." Jamison put his hands back on my knees, slid them up the insides of my thighs once again, parting my legs wider than before. "Are you wet for us?"

 ENNY

AND THOSE WORDS ruined my panties and made me realize I'd analyze whatever it was between us later. Much, much later.

The feel of Boone's attentions on my neck and the placement of Jamison's fingers had my mind going blank. I could only feel.

"Are you nervous?" Boone asked.

I blinked my eyes open once again, turned my head. He was still beside me, but several inches separated us now. I frowned. "No."

"Have you been kissed before?"

"Yes."

"Has a man ever touched you, like this?" Jamison

asked, his fingers creeping a little closer to my pussy and I squeezed my legs together.

He pulled them away entirely, misinterpreting my action as disinterest, when, in fact, I'd wanted to pin his hands in place.

"No," I said. I stood up, forcing Jamison to slide back on the coffee table to make room for me. I took a deep breath. Let it out. Practically stomped my boot on the floor. "You guys were all hot for me before you found out I'm a virgin. Now it's like you think I'm going to break or burst into tears or something. The only difference between us is that you've done this before. You've got experience. I'm not any less eager and if you saw the state of my panties, you'd know that. I'm not going to break."

"Kitten does have claws," Boone said, the corner of his mouth tipped up. "All right, one last question."

I quirked a brow, waited.

"If you've never had a man touch you, then have you ever made yourself come?"

I felt my cheeks heat, but knew I couldn't go all virgin-like on them now. No, I wanted them, wanted *this*. "Yes."

Jamison's hand dropped to the thick length in his pants and he shifted on the coffee table. He couldn't be comfortable.

"Show us," Boone said.

I looked between them and they only watched me. Waited. If I was going to do this, I needed to pull up my big-girl panties and get to it. Although, I doubted those panties would be on for very long.

Inwardly, I smiled and sat back down on the couch, leaned back and parted my legs. This was just like in my bed in the dark. Alone. Yeah, not at all. The lights were on and I had two virile men watching the path of my hand as I slid it down my belly and over my jean skirt. Their deep breathing were the only sounds in the room. Their gazes heated me in ways a roaring fire in the cold fireplace never could.

Parting my legs slightly, the skirt rode up a little.

Jamison patted his knees. "Put your feet here."

I lifted one, put it on his right knee. He took hold of the boot, tugged it off, dropped it to the floor with a thud. Slid the cream-colored knee-high sock off, let it fall. I lifted the other foot and he did the same, then placed both of my bare feet on his knees.

Slowly, he widened his legs which made my feet go further and further apart, and my skirt rode up so it was around my hips. A very intentional action that was sexy and tawdry and I loved it. I bit my lip to stifle a whimper and watched them watch me. My panties, specifically, as if they were the hottest thing they'd ever seen.

"You are wet," Jamison said, his eyes focused squarely between my legs. The dark stubble on his jaw caught the light and I couldn't miss the hints of red. "So wet the lace is clinging to your pussy."

"Take them off," Boone uttered. I had to wonder if that was his command voice used in the ER when needed. The dark tone was delicious and hit some hot buttons I didn't even know I had. Some would say I had a submissive nature since I hooked my thumbs into the sides of my panties, and did exactly what he said.

I lifted my hips and worked them down to my knees, Jamison claiming them there and working them off the rest of the way. Instead of dropping them to the floor like my boots and socks, he tucked the tiny thong into his shirt pocket.

I bit my lip as they continued to stare, this time at my bare pussy. No man had seen it before and I felt exposed and...nervous. Was mine normal? Appealing?

"You are so beautiful," Boone said, his eyes narrowed in what I would have assumed to be anger, but he was just aroused. Impressively so. His jaw clenched at it seemed he had to concentrate to relax. "Everywhere."

"Touch that gorgeous pussy," Jamison added.

From their heated gazes, I felt pretty, felt desired. That I held some kind of power over them was exhilarating. I placed my hand over my folds, discovered myself wetter than I'd ever been before. I moved my fingertips directly to my clit, which was hard and almost throbbing. My eyes fell closed at the feel of it, and knowing they were watching me felt wicked.

I gasped and my eyes flew open when I was touched, just below my fingers. Boone had leaned in and had one finger on me. With his other hand, he lifted mine away, brought it to his mouth and licked my fingertips clean.

The feel of his tongue swirling over them like an ice cream cone, knowing he was tasting my arousal, had my mouth fall open in surprise. It was so carnal, especially the way his gaze bored into me. As if he planned to devour every inch of me, and was starting with my fingers.

"Sweet," he murmured.

Jamison growled as he hooked behind my knees and dropped to the floor between my thighs. "I want a taste."

I didn't even have a chance to think about more than the feel of my calves over his shoulders when he put his mouth on me. There.

"Oh god!" I cried out, my hips bucking of their own volition. His mouth slid over me, top to bottom and back, lapping up my wetness, learning every inch of me. At first, it was with the flat of his tongue, then he firmed it, flicked it over and around the sensitive left side of my clit. I felt the rasp of his beard on the inside of my thighs, adding another sensation to the onslaught.

He pulled back, licked his lips. "So fucking sweet. Sticky, like honey." With one hand on the back of my thigh, holding me nice and wide for him, his other fingers slid over me, circled my entrance.

"Any guy ever touch you here?"

I saw his finger circle around my pink flesh, could hear the sound of just how wet I was from just the small motion. It was so carnal, the sight. His blunt finger... there. I didn't wax like some women I knew. I shaved, kept things tidy and trimmed, but had never considered what a man might like.

"No." When I shook my head, my hair slid over the soft cushion. I was close to coming, just from the teasing licks he'd given me. It wasn't enough. I needed more. Reaching up, I stroked my hand through his short hair, tugged him closer.

"Good." He circled my opening one more time, then dipped in. His eyes narrowed and I heard him groan, a deep rumbling from his chest. "Watch how you take my finger. That's it. So fucking tight. Greedy, too. That's right, grab hold and pull me in. Imagine how it's going to be with a nice big dick."

He kept talking to me, saying dirty things as he gently finger fucked me. My hips began to move, as if my body somehow knew how to get him to go faster, deeper. Just right.

Boone put a forearm on the back of the couch above me, leaned forward and put his hand on my lower belly. The denim and my shirt blocked skin to skin touch, at least until he slid down and his thumb zeroed in on my clit. Now both of them were touching me, working my pussy in tandem.

Both were watching me closely, studying my responses to their actions and seemed to adjust their small movements accordingly. I couldn't remain still, my hips lifting and curling as I got closer and closer to coming. I knew what I wanted, an orgasm. And Jamison and Boone were going to give me one. A big, explosive, mind-blowing, insane orgasm that was going to ruin me for my own hand, my vibrator and any other man.

I bit my lip.

"We want to hear you, Kitten," Jamison said, sliding his finger out and I whimpered, but he added a second, carefully working both of them in.

I was so tight and his fingers stretched me open. I knew he was doing it in preparation for what came next... their cocks.

"Yes!" I cried when he curled those fingers just right and my hips flew up off the couch. It was as if I had some kind of hot button inside me that set off my orgasm. With Boone's thumb, the combination was just...bliss.

My head pressed into the couch cushion, I tensed, my thighs pressing into Jamison's shoulders. I wasn't quiet as the most incredible orgasm rocked me...and rocked me. And *rocked me.*

Neither let up and it went on and on. Eventually, I caught my breath, slumped into the couch. Sweaty, replete and I couldn't help the smile that formed on my lips. *That* was what I'd been missing.

"So beautiful," Boone murmured. I opened my eyes and caught them both licking their fingers clean. They sure liked to taste me. "Now we've got you all soft and relaxed for our dicks."

Jamison lowered my legs from his shoulders and settled back onto the coffee table again. He helped me to stand directly before him, my skirt still hitched up above my waist.

"Ready for more?" he asked, his heated gaze looking me over. I was sure I looked like a disheveled, well pleasured mess.

My hair was probably snarled, my cheeks flushed and I was boldly bare from the waist down. And I didn't care.

"Oh yes," I replied, the smile not slipping from my face. I had a feeling it was going to be there for a while.

Jamison grinned and his fingers went to the button on my skirt, worked the denim down and off my hips. I was impatient, eager for more. That orgasm was addictive, like a hit of some powerful drug. I knew all the scientific terms behind *why* I felt so good, but who cared? Not me. All I knew was that I wanted another Boone and Jamison induced orgasm. Now.

I undid the buttons on my blouse with steady fingers,

shrugged it off, then reached behind me, unhooked my bra and dropped it to the floor as well.

I was before them, naked. Exposed. Vulnerable. Yet *very* horny.

But the way they looked at me, the way their hands came up and gently brushed over my bare skin had me feeling...pretty, too.

"Look at you," Boone said, his knuckles stroking down over my hip, the full curve of my bottom. He was so big, so...brawny and yet I felt cherished, not vulnerable as I had with the asshole at the bar. "So fucking beautiful."

And I didn't feel like an easy lay. I may have only known them an obscenely short time and now I was naked before them—and well sated by an orgasm they'd easily wrung from my body—what we were doing felt special. Important.

"I'm short."

"A tiny, gorgeous package," Jamison countered.

"Curvy."

"Fucking perfect," Boone added. He turned me to him, cupped my breasts.

"They're big." I was expressing every one of my hang-ups. My double-Ds were disproportionately large for my height. Running wasn't something I did without two sports bras...and only if being chased by an axe murderer.

His thumbs slid back and forth over my nipples, watching as they hardened into hard points. The action felt so good, as if there was a direct link between what he was doing and my clit. He looked at me almost reverently. "I'm a breast man, Kitten."

Jamison gave me a swat on the butt and I startled, pressing myself into Boone's hands. "And I'm an ass man," Jamison commented as he stroked over the heated skin. "Like that, did you?"

I didn't respond because I realized I had. While the slight spank had been a surprise, the sting morphed into heat and I felt myself get wetter...if that were even possible. He gave me another little spank, prompting me into a response.

"Yes," I gasped. "I'm big other places, too," I admitted and for once I was thankful my pale skin was already flushed. I bit my lip, realizing maybe this flaw wasn't something I should point out.

Jamison quirked a brow.

I lowered my hand between my thighs, felt how swollen I was. How wet. How sensitive. "Here. My...lips here are large."

Boone huffed out a breath. "More of you to wrap around our dicks." When I didn't respond, he went on. "I'm a doctor and that's my expert opinion."

I couldn't help but smile, felt my irrational issues slip away.

"I like that I can see your clit from here, all pink and hard for us," Jamison added. "As for big? I just had an up-close and personal look at your pussy, tasted it even, Kitten, and it's nothing less than perfect."

They didn't seem bothered by any of my hang-ups. Well, they were *bothered,* but everything I considered personal flaws was appealing to them.

"Oh, Kitten, what we're going to do to you," Boone said before tossing me over his shoulder and carrying me up the stairs and dropping me onto a soft bed. "That orgasm was just a warm-up. Before we're done with you, you won't even remember your name."

They stood at the foot of the bed, eyeing me with narrowed, heated gazes. I couldn't miss the thick outlines of their erections in their jeans. They'd been focused solely on me, keeping their needs in check. I liked them this way, but had to imagine what they would be like when their needs were set free. I didn't want them to be careful with me. Jamison's spanks had been playful, their touches gentle. It was a side of them I liked, but I wanted more. I wanted the wild. The rugged. The dark.

"Promises, promises," I replied coyly, planting my feet on the bed and spreading my knees wide.

Their hands dropped to their jeans, working them off their narrow hips just enough so their cocks sprang free. Oh, shit. Now I knew why Jamison's cock looked like a steel beam down his thigh and Boone wasn't any smaller. Thick and long, the flesh of their dicks was darker, redder than the rest of them. A thick vein ran up the underside of Jamison's cock and Boone's was crowned with a wide head, a pearly drop of fluid sliding down. Both bobbed upward toward their bellies.

My pussy clenched at the thought of being opened up by such massive cocks. Jamison's finger felt good, but those...those clubs? My legs had started to come together as I was beginning to second guess my taunt when they pounced.

8

OONE

I WAS A DOCTOR. I'd seen females naked before. I wasn't a monk either. I'd fucked my way through my twenties, had been much more selective in my thirties. But no one compared to Penny. Holy. Fucking. Shit.

She was sweet. Smart. A little sassy. Bold. Passionate. And when she parted those silky soft thighs, she also had a very naughty streak. And she topped it with a cherry.

Fuck, my balls were primed to come. I could feel the need at the base of my spine, the tingle, the pressure to just sink into her and explode. And I'd only felt her up, nothing more. When I was sixteen, I'd gotten my hands on my first pair of tits and I'd done just that, making a mess of my pants and a fool of myself. I had more control now...I hoped.

If she wanted to get dirty, we'd give it to her, but this first time, we'd take her the way she deserved. She was giving us a fucking gift.

I started shucking my clothes, toeing off my boots as I undid the buttons on my shirt. Five seconds were wasted on getting naked, but I kept my eyes on Kitten the whole time, taking in every inch of her spread out on my bed. She was just where I'd dreamed...hoped, since the first second I saw her. Her pale hair fanned out beneath her, the wide-eyed, eager gaze as she watched us strip. The perfect swells of her breasts, topped with pale pink nipples, already hard. The soft curve of her belly, wide hips, toned legs. And between them? The most perfect pussy I'd ever seen. She was a natural blonde and the pale hair couldn't hide her pink lips, all swollen and wet.

Jamison had had a taste of her. I licked my lips, ready for my turn.

"We need to make sure you're ready, all nice and relaxed, your pussy all slick and soft for our big dicks," I told her, seeing Jamison nod as he worked off his shirt at a much slower pace.

She shifted on the bed, her feet sliding on the sheets. "I'm ready. Really."

Slowly, I shook my head. "Not yet."

I reached forward, grabbed both her ankles and pulled her to the very edge of the bed. She squeaked in surprise, then came up on her elbows so she could look at me. I fell to my knees on the soft carpet, put my hands on the silkiest fucking inner thighs I'd ever felt, held her open as I put my mouth on her. Took a deep breath, breathed her in. Felt her hot, sweet honey coat my tongue, my lips, even my whiskers.

I groaned.

She moaned. Gripped handfuls of the sheet.

"She tastes so fucking good, doesn't she?" Jamison asked.

The sound of his boots hitting the floor one after the other followed, but I didn't answer, too busy sucking on her plump folds, flicking over her clit with my tongue. All that did was have her hands move to my hair and tug. Her eyes fell closed and she flopped back on the bed.

"I'm ready. I'm ready," she repeated again and again as I got her closer to the brink. I had no intention of pushing her over. I knew I could, but that was the perk of being older and more skilled. I'd take her right to the edge and leave her there so that when Jamison filled her up for the first time, she'd come instead of hurting.

I was careful with her, flicking at her little bud with precision as I slipped one finger into her, trying to let her get used to something inside her. She was so fucking wet that I added a second finger, scissored them to stretch her untried tissues and she quivered and clenched around me, tight. So fucking tight.

"Please, Boone. Please fuck me."

I growled then, licked her from ass to clit one last time and sat back on my heels. Pre-cum slid in a steady stream down my shaft, coating my balls. Looking up, I saw the way Kitten was lost, completely given over to her need, to what I'd wrung from her body.

I nodded to Jamison as I stood, moved to the head of the bed and settled into the pile of pillows as Jamison scooped Kitten up, laid her against me so she was leaning back against my chest. Reaching around, I cupped her breasts, kissed the side of her neck and up to her ear.

I shifted, hooked my heels on the inside of her calves, spread our legs wide as Jamison moved into position between her parted thighs. He knelt, stroked his hand over her tender flesh.

"It's time, Kitten. Do you want Jamison to fill you up? Take that sweet cherry?"

"Please," she whimpered. Her nipples were hard points against my palms, her skin dewy with perspiration, her pussy all swollen and eager. I breathed in the scent of her arousal, licked my lips at the lingering taste. Felt the sticky honey on the tips of my fingers.

"You're ours, Penelope Vandervelk," Jamison said, his voice a dark rumble, his need so great as he lined himself up with her virgin opening.

"Ours," I repeated as I watched my friend slide into Kitten and claim her.

PENNY

THEY WERE GOOD. Really, *really* good at this. I was so far gone with my need that while I felt Jamison's dick sliding in—how could I miss something the size of a steel beam stretching me wider and wider still—I was too eager for it to be panicked.

I wanted Jamison in me. Needed it. Somehow, I felt

empty without one, which was crazy since I'd never had one in me before.

A whimper slipped past my lips as Jamison slid back, pushed forward, a fraction of an inch at a time. As he did so, Boone played with my breasts, plucking and tugging on my nipples, nipping along my neck and whispering praise and dark promises in my ear.

Only one dick could take my virginity. Maybe Jamison won a coin toss; I had no idea, but Boone wasn't going to just sit on the sidelines and watch. No, he was actively involved. I could feel the hard press of his cock at my back, knew he'd have his turn next, but he was in on this whole virginity-taking thing too.

"Good girl. Watch, Kitten. Watch as that tight pussy swallows Jamison's dick."

Jamison had one hand on the headboard well over Boone's head, the other between my legs, a finger sliding carefully around my entrance, those big lips down there that really did wrap around a dick.

My eyes flicked up to Jamison's, his lids lowered, his jaw clenched. Sweat dripped down his temple. He was holding back. I could see the tense lines of his body, felt the careful thrusts, knew that this wasn't normal, what he needed.

"More," I told him. Yes, I was giving him my virginity, but both of us were in this. "I want this to be good for you, too."

Jamison laughed, but it was jagged. "Kitten, if it were any better, I'd probably have an aneurysm."

"Then why aren't you moving harder? Deeper?"

Perhaps his hips moved of their own volition, but he

slid in another inch and I felt the stretch, the burn of it and I hissed.

"That's why. You're so tight. So wet. You're like a fist, a fucking vise."

He wasn't going to do it. Somehow, he was afraid to hurt me. Even with his need being so desperate, he was thinking of me. I'd told them earlier, I wasn't breakable. Sure, that pesky hymen was, but that stupid thing didn't dictate how this went. I did. Well, *they* did, but in this moment, I could take the control. Could do what Jamison refused, even if it came close to killing him.

I lifted my hips in one strong surge, Jamison sliding all the way in.

Jamison groaned, his hand moving away and slapping the bed beside my hip.

Boone whispered, "Fuck."

I cried out at Jamison filling me completely. They were right. He fit. But my inner walls were rippling, trying to adjust to the invasion.

Boone's hands gentled, his words soothing as they let me adjust.

"Kitten," Jamison scolded as he tried to catch his breath.

"There, it's done," I breathed. "Now show me how good it can be."

I met Jamison's gray eyes as I gave him the challenge. He grinned in return.

"Yes, ma'am."

He began to move then, deep, slow strokes in and out as he watched me, making sure I was okay. But I liked this pace, the way every single nerve ending inside me came awake.

"Oh my god."

Jamison grinned even wider. "Just wait."

He must have been satisfied by what he felt, what he saw on my face, because he hooked my knee and lifted it up so he had a different angle.

My eyes flared wide at the deeper penetration.

"Wait until you feel this pussy, Boone. So hot, so wet. She fits like a glove. I'm molding her pussy to fit my dick. Your turn's next."

It was as if a lead had snapped and Jamison gave up all pretense of control. He fucked hard, deep. The sound of our flesh slapping together merged with our ragged breathing.

"Time to come, Kitten," Boone murmured in my ear as he continued to play with my breasts.

I had no idea how he could tell just by looking at me, but he was right. With Jamison's precision fucking, Boone's playful hands, the pleasure was coming from everywhere. My ears tingled, my toes curled. My pussy throbbed, pulsed. My clit ached.

It all coalesced into this bright white brilliance and I came, my body going tense, my breath caught in my throat as it took me under.

Neither stopped what they were doing as I came. And came. I caught my breath and cried out, gripped Boone's hard thighs, pressed my head into his shoulder.

I felt Jamison grow even larger inside me before he pounded into me, once, twice, then groaned, the reverberations of it coming from deep in his chest. His butt was taut as he came. I could feel the heat of his cum as he filled me up. My orgasm had lingered, but I knew my pussy was milking him, taking all of that cum deep.

Jamison lifted his head. His eyes were this blurry haze. Gone was the tension, the desperate need. Now, it showed happiness. Male satisfaction. This was the look of a well-fucked male, of a man just finished with the most elemental of tasks. Fucking, mating, filling a female with his seed.

He sat back on his heels, carefully pulling his cock from me. I saw that it was still hard, still a dark plum color, but now it glistened with our combined fluids. Jamison looked down at himself.

"That's hot as fuck," he murmured, then shifted his gaze to my parted thighs. I felt the hot gush of his cum as it slipped from me. His finger gentle slid over my sensitive folds. "This, too."

His eyes raked up my body, met mine. "I took you bare. I assume you're not on anything."

I shook my head. I'd never gone on the pill because I never intended to sleep around. I knew that when I gave myself to a man that he would be the One, that I wouldn't want anything between us. No latex. Nothing. Just skin on skin.

I just never imagined the One would be two.

"I've never fucked without a condom, Kitten. You're the first. The last. You wanted forever." He collected his cum, worked it back inside me and I whimpered at the feel of it. "There's no going back now."

No, there wasn't. I felt his cum. There was so much of it and I knew it was deep inside me. So deep he could give me the forever I wanted. A baby. A family of my own.

"My turn, Kitten," Boone said, moving his hands from my breasts to my hips.

With ease that proved he was so very strong, and I was so very small, he had me spun about with easy motions. I leaned down, kissed him, felt every hard inch of his hot body pressing against mine.

The kiss was a wild tangle of our tongues as his hands cupped my bottom, held me against him.

"Straddle me," he said when he broke the kiss.

I bent my knees, put them on either side of his hips, and he helped me to sit up. His cock was right in front of me, rising straight up. He gripped the base in one hand, stroked it once. Twice. A pearly drop of fluid appeared at the tip.

Jamison knelt on the side of the bed, took my hand and helped me so I was up on my knees.

"That's it. Now take Boone in. He wants some of that perfect pussy, too."

I flicked my gaze at Boone who had more restraint, more patience than anyone I met. But I knew he could only last for so long. I lowered myself, shifted my hips until he nudged me, sliding easily over my folds that were coated now in Jamison's cum. He settled at my entrance.

"Take me deep," Boone instructed. "It should be nice and easy this time. No pain and all that cum to make it a slippery ride."

Gravity helped, too. Once the broad crown stretched me open, I lowered onto him in one easy slide. This angle was different. Deeper and I felt him bump the end of me.

I leaned forward, placed my hands on his bare shoulders to change the angle, to ease the slight bite of pain.

Boone's hands went to my hips and Jamison moved away, watched.

"Fuck, yes. I love it that we're bare. That I'm taking you raw, the only thing between us is Jamison's cum. Don't worry, I'll get mine in you, too. Nice and full."

I shivered at his dirty words, the promises in them.

"Remember that wild ride we promised? Go for it."

Boone lifted me, lowered me back down, let me see what it felt like, what I should do, but I quickly got the hang of it. It wasn't Boone who was fucking me, but the other way around. I was riding him, using his dick for my pleasure. But in this position, I could rub my clit, circle my hips so that I was on the brink of coming in a matter of seconds.

"Wow. Okay, um...am I supposed to come again?" I asked, as if I weren't supposed to keep enjoying myself.

Boone grinned. "You fucking better."

I couldn't help but smile at his threat and took him in earnest. I was panting, my eyes closed, hair long down my back as I got lost in the pleasure. "I'm almost there. I can't... I need—"

Before I could tell Boone what I needed, he rolled us so he was on top, my head on his pillow as he took over. Taking my ankles, he lifted them to his shoulders. Fucked me hard. He leaned forward so I was almost bent in half. One hand slid over my clit, then moved around to my ass and I tensed, clenched down. Came.

"Oh. My. God!" I cried out. The slightest caress of his finger on my back entrance had somehow pushed me over the edge and I let go. I couldn't keep quiet, couldn't do anything but give over to it, to whatever Boone wanted to do to me. I didn't care what it was. I was too far gone to be embarrassed, concerned or modest.

When I finally caught my breath, I was a sweaty, wilted mess. Boone was still thick and hard in me when he pulled out. I gasped at the emptiness, but he spun me about once again. He hadn't come and seemed far from done. "Grab the headboard."

With unsteady hands, I did as he said, then he hooked an arm about my waist. I felt the thick prod of him at my entrance just before he slid back into me again.

"Oh!" I cried.

His hands settled on top of mine, and I felt the soft hairs of his chest tickle my back as he kissed my neck, nipped my ear. "My turn to take you for a wild ride."

He did just that, fucking me like a stallion does a mare. Hard, deep, flesh slapping flesh. Sweaty skin clinging. Groans and pants filling the room.

I came again at some point, but I was too far gone to do more than whimper, clench his dick.

Boone came...finally, with a shout and a deep thrust, his cock embedded in me so deep I wasn't sure where he finished off and I began.

Fingers worked mine from the headboard and I was lowered to the soft mattress, Boone's body pressing into me from behind, his dick still deep inside me. I felt the soft stroke of a hand brushing my hair from my sweaty face.

"Sleep, Kitten. You're going to need it."

And so I did. And Boone was right. I did need it

because I woke up to Boone fucking me as we lay like two spoons in a drawer before carrying me into the shower so Jamison could soap me all up, drop to his knees and clean my pussy with his mouth. Before dawn, Jamison rolled me onto my back and fucked me slow and deep. After that, I remembered nothing but the hot, slick feel of their cum coating my thighs, the tender burn of being so well-used. The touch of their bodies as they held me.

9

P ENNY

"THAT'S PROBABLY Kady and her men," Jamison said when the doorbell rang.

"What?" I screeched.

We were sprawled on his supersized couch, my head in Boone's lap, my feet over Jamison's thighs. We were watching a series on satellite and had made it as far as the second episode. To say I was tired—and a little sore—was an understatement and the fact that I was vegging out in the middle of the day was proof of it.

"Now? Here?" I spun in a circle between the couch and the coffee table, panicking. I had no idea what to do. Boone grunted when I pushed off his belly with my elbow and Jamison deflected a heel kick to the crotch.

"They got back this morning from their trip and went

out to the ranch. Riley called earlier wondering where you were."

I put my hands on my hips, narrowed my eyes. "Why didn't you tell me?"

This was my *sister*. Well, half-sister, but still. I hadn't even known she'd existed until a few weeks ago. And now she was ringing Boone's doorbell because she wanted to meet me. Oh. My. God.

"Because, Kitten," Jamison began, cutting into my irrational thoughts. "You and Boone were in the shower and I could hear you coming from the kitchen."

I couldn't help but blush, remembering exactly what Boone had done when he'd dropped to his knees and put my foot up on the built-in shower bench. My pussy clenched at his very thorough attentions at getting me clean...with his mouth. It seemed both men liked playing in the shower.

The doorbell rang again. I whipped around to face the direction of the front door.

"What if she hates me?" I took a deep breath, let it out, trying to calm my crazy heart. It was practically beating out of my chest. "Or worse, what if she's a total bitch?" I whispered the last, worried she might hear me from two rooms away and through a thick door.

Both men smiled and began to laugh, but when I narrowed my gaze and gave them the look of death, they stifled them.

"Kitten, Kady is not a bitch," Jamison said, his voice reassuring. "You're going to get along great...if you'd just open the door."

"What, like this?" I asked, holding my arms out to

indicate I was wearing only one of Boone's flannel shirts and my knee-high socks. The tails of the shirt hung several inches lower than my jean skirt from the night before, brushing over my knees. I'd rolled the sleeves up three times. It was practically a muumuu on me.

"I don't think she cares what you're wearing."

There was pounding on the door followed by shouting. "Boone, open this door! I know my sister is in there. I want to meet her. RIGHT. NOW!"

My mouth fell open and I froze. That was her voice. My sister. She was pissed.

Boone stood and pointed in the direction of the banging. "Don't mess with that one. She taught third grade, I think."

"Second," Jamison corrected. "Although she's teaching middle school here in Barlow."

"Even worse, those little buggers." He winked and headed toward the door.

Realizing he was going to open it and not me, I leapt over the coffee table and sprinted, all but knocking Boone out of the way to beat him to it.

I yanked open the door, let it bounce off the stopper as I stood and stared. And stared. I knew there were two men behind her. I could see them, but I paid them no mind. If a judge asked me what they looked like, I wouldn't be able to give a description. I was that blinded by my sister.

"You look nothing like me," I said, my tone full of surprise and awe as I took her in.

She was at least six inches taller, had fiery red hair

and a peaches and cream complexion. She wore a cute green sundress and heeled sandals. She was...lovely.

"I always wanted blonde hair," she replied.

Her arms were wrapped around me in a fierce hug before I even realized it and it took me a second to lift my arms and hug her back. She smelled of a light perfume, something floral or citrusy.

Now I took in the two men behind her. One was huge. Like football linebacker enormous. I had to wonder if he ate whole chickens or small African villages for dinner. The other guy was just as tall, but built much more average-sized. At least by Montana standards. The only two sizes of men here were Big and Bigger.

Their eyes were squarely on the back of Kady's head and the looks on their rugged faces softened with something akin to reverence. *Love.* That's what it was. Kady was happy, so they were happy.

Was Kady happy? She was crying, I could feel her body shaking.

"Hey," I said, pulling back and putting my hands on her upper arms so I could meet her eyes. "Why are you crying?"

I wasn't a crier and wasn't overly emotional. Perhaps it was my nature, or perhaps it was because I'd learned to mute my emotions or I'd have been a total wreck.

She laughed, wiping her eyes with the back of her hands. "If you can't tell, I'm a girlie girl. This is what I do."

I'd thought I was high-maintenance, my mother drilling pride in my appearance since I was old enough to tie my own shoes. But being a scientist, especially one in the oil and gas field, I knew how to get dirty, was used to wearing mud-soaked jeans and rubber boots. And now I stood before her in just a shirt and knee-highs. I'd never gotten conditioner in my hair in the shower and it was all flyaway tangles. I looked...well-fucked. Far from appropriate to have visitors.

But Kady? She was all pretty curls and hot pink toenail polish.

"I've been waiting for you," she said, sniffling and smiling. "God, I've been stuck in Montana with a bunch of men."

"Sweetness, you weren't complaining last night, stuck between *two* men," one of them said.

Kady's cheeks turned bright red as she rolled her eyes. She turned, held out her arm. "This is Cord and Riley. My men."

"Ma'am," the bigger one said, eyeing my attire but making no mention of it.

"It's great to put a face with a whole bunch of paperwork," the other one added with a smile. Riley Townsend. The lawyer.

"Let's let them in the front door, Kitten," Boone murmured from behind me.

I stepped back and Boone led them into the great room. Jamison shook the other men's hands. He eyed me, then Kady. "Boone has a new camper. Have you seen it?"

"I heard about the ATV," Cord said, rubbing his hands together.

Boone cocked his head. "I'll show you both and give the ladies some time to get to know each other."

He winked, then led the men through the kitchen and

into the garage. When the door slammed shut, Kady spun to me, took my hands.

"Talk."

I frowned. "About what specifically?" We had our whole lives to catch up on. Where was I to start?

"About why you're wearing a man's flannel shirt and not much else. Why you're here with Boone *and* Jamison. And don't tell me you guys played Scrabble."

"Is it that obvious I'm not wearing a bra?"

She shook her head. "Only because I've got big boobs, too. I'm in the club."

"I better get dressed," I said, turning toward the bedroom.

"I'm coming with you." She tagged along right behind me.

I found my clothes neatly folded on an overstuffed chair beneath the large window. The bed had been made. There were no signs of any kind of sexy times whatsoever, bless Boone's OCD heart. It made the pseudo walk-of-shame a little easier.

"What's this about Scrabble?"

She laughed, crossed her arms over her chest. "Jamison and I played Scrabble one night. He's ruthless. Fair warning."

"Huh." I thought of him playing the board game. It seemed I had much to learn about him. About both of my men.

"By the way you're blushing, I'd say no Scrabble. I want details," she said, sitting down on the corner of the bed.

"Don't you want to know about my middle school years or when I got my ears pierced?" I countered.

She shrugged. "Later. I want the juicy stuff first."

I carried everything into the bathroom, set them on the counter. I didn't close the door, but got changed with a little bit of privacy. I stripped and put on my underwear. My skirt. "I'm sure you can guess. I'm in Boone's house, wearing his shirt."

"Cute knee highs," she commented as I put on my own shirt. "I slept with Cord and Riley the day we met."

My fingers stilled on the buttons. I turned and stood in the doorway at that bombshell. "You did?"

She gave me a sly smile and her cheeks turned pink. Nodded. "And by *slept* I mean had wild monkey sex on the front porch of the main house."

My mouth fell open thinking of that porch. Of sweet Kady getting it on outside like that. With both of those big cowboys. It seemed Kady had an inner slut, and that meant that it was okay for me to wonder about mine. To know that it was okay to have one.

"Oh. Um...wow."

I couldn't think of anything else to say. I was highly educated and she'd reduced me to single syllables.

"And you?" Her eyebrow went up and she stared at me with mischievous green eyes.

I went back to work on the buttons so I didn't have to look at her as I responded. "Well...um, I met them the other day, when I first arrived. Met all the guys from the ranch. Just a quick introduction, nothing more. I didn't see them again—Jamison and Boone—until last night at the Silky Spur. I...um, I don't really understand it. *Us.* It's a little crazy. I mean, I had sex with them after knowing them only about an hour."

She stood, waved her had in the air as if it were nothing.

"The way they look at you?" She fanned herself with her hand. "It's obvious they really want you. And I don't mean for sexy times."

I'd never really talked to anyone about sex, or my lack of having it. It had gotten to a point where I'd gotten too old to have the conversation. Every friend in college had had sex before and me asking them questions was too little, too late. And it wasn't as if my mother had talked to me about sex. She'd only told me never to disgrace the family. That I had to be discreet in everything I did.

I'd made out with two men in a gas station, then slept with them—and by *slept* I didn't mean sleep—and then wasn't discreet about it in the slightest when answering Boone's door in just his shirt.

"I...um, I've never done it before. Last night was my first time."

Kady's mouth fell open but then she cocked her head to the side, smiled at me in a wistful way. "How sweet that it was with them. I bet those two went all alpha male on you with that one."

I couldn't help but laugh. "Oh yeah."

"Did they make it good for you?" she asked, then waved her hand through the air again. "Never mind. Of course, they did. If they're anything like my men, then they had you come at least once before they even got inside you, right?"

It was now my turn to blush. I had no intention of

telling her we hadn't used any protection, that they might have gotten me pregnant. That I might be excited about the possibility. I wasn't ready to explain all of that to her. Not now.

"Are you okay?" she asked. "Emotionally, I mean."

"Yes."

"It wasn't a one-night stand," she said, as if she knew this for fact. I might have slept with Boone and Jamison, but she'd known them longer. "I'm sure you're worried about that, even if they've said otherwise. I heard about your Masters. Congratulations. That means you're one smart cookie and you'll probably analyze all this to pieces. I know I did, and I didn't have the whole virginity thing to deal with. Whatever they say, believe them. They want you, seriously want you, or you wouldn't be here."

"They said they wanted forever."

She bit her lip and tears came to her eyes. "God, that's so sweet. We're trying to have a baby," she admitted.

Baby? My cell rang from my purse. I went to the chair and pulled it out, saw it was my mother. I swiped the screen to dismiss the call, put the phone away. "Sorry, my mother."

"You don't get along with her?"

"No. That conversation is best served with a bottle of wine. Maybe two." I wasn't going to say more about my mother. Not now. I was too overwhelmed with everything else. Boone and Jamison. Them wanting forever. Meeting Kady. "So, a baby?" I asked instead, turning the conversation back to her.

She stood, went over to the window, nodded. Cord

was riding Boone's ATV across the big back yard. "Boys and their toys."

She looked at Cord the same way he'd looked at her earlier. Wistfully.

"You love them."

She nodded. "Oh yes. Would you believe me if I said it was love at first sight, with both of them?"

With my eyes, I followed Cord and the ATV back and forth across the yard. If we'd had this conversation before I'd met Jamison and Boone, I'd have probably said yes just to make her feel good. But now? Now I believed it one hundred percent. What else could this be? The attraction, the need, the desire to just be with them, it had to be love. I'd told them my deepest secrets and dreams, given them my virginity and even made myself susceptible to so much more than heartbreak. But I knew. I *knew* they wouldn't hurt me. Stupid, my mother would say. Perhaps I was being stupid. But I was stupid in love and I wasn't going to waste it. Wasn't going to run away from it just because it might go bad, that it might be inappropriate that I wanted two men.

I might be a Vandervelk on paper, but my DNA screamed Steele.

"Absolutely," I told her.

"That's why we're trying for a baby. I want one. I always have. Them, too, it seems. Well, at least they want one with me." Her hand slid over her flat belly. "I'm excited."

"Based on what Cord said in the doorway, the three of you are trying pretty hard."

She grinned wickedly. "I was on the pill, but I stopped

a few weeks ago. It might take a while, but they're willing to put their best efforts into it."

I thought of Boone and Jamison, of how they'd taken me without protection. They'd been like two cavemen, seeing their cum slip from me. The idea of them making a baby with me had only made them hard again, which made them fuck me again and fill me with more cum. I wasn't sure how I *wasn't* pregnant. If Kady's men were as virile, as attentive, she was probably pregnant now. Maybe that was why she was so weepy.

"You have the main house now to yourself, although if your men are anything like mine, you won't be staying there all too much."

We hadn't spoken of next steps, nothing more than forever. Boone had a shift at the ER tomorrow and while the ranch would probably survive without Jamison, he couldn't shirk his duties because of me for very long. While I wanted a family, a house to take care of, I didn't think the men meant Boone's house, nor beginning immediately.

"I assume we'll be dating, having more quiet times on the couch watching movies. Months of getting to know each other. I'll be back at the main house by dinner. Alone."

She laughed, then stopped when I wasn't laughing with her. Instead, I frowned.

"I'm sorry, but you're serious, aren't you?"

I realized I hadn't finished buttoning my shirt and did them up as I replied. "Yes, I'm serious. I have stuff to resolve." I pointed at my purse. "My mother is going to hound me about something. Most likely the outline for my dissertation or the job offers she's somehow heard about. I swear she has my email bugged."

"Isn't she a congresswoman?"

"Yup," I said, tucking my shirt into my jean skirt. "And she's not thrilled I'm here. Aiden Steele is her dirty laundry. The sooner I'm out of Montana, the better."

"What?" She gripped my forearm. "You're not leaving, are you?"

"I have no intention of going anywhere. I like it here. I like Jamison and Boone. I *really* like what we did last night."

She waggled her red eyebrows and grinned.

I smiled. "I just have to figure out my stuff. It's not like I've known about the inheritance for very long."

She offered me a small smile in return. "Well, I'm glad you're here. I have a half-sister, Beth, who I grew up with. She's...she's a drug addict and in a locked-down rehab." She sighed. "We'll need something even stronger than wine for that topic. What I'm telling you is I miss having a sister."

Now I felt wistful because she was actually interested in me. "I have a half-sister I grew up with, too. Evelyn. She's six years older. I was shipped off to boarding school when I was eleven—"

"Like Harry Potter? I'm a teacher, remember, so I know everything about the series."

I thought of Chapman Academy, about my years there. My mother got her money's worth out of the place, but I'd gotten more out of it than just the fancy education. I'd learned just how little I'd been wanted. I'd been like the fancy silver, pulled out for special occasions, then put away once the need for me was over. "No flying brooms, unfortunately. Evelyn and I were never close. She's a lawyer now in North Carolina. So yes, I'm glad I'm here, too. With you."

She slung her arm over my shoulders and we looked out the window. Boone, Jamison and Riley were standing together talking, all manly and a feast for the eyes. The loud motor of the ATV came first, then Cord flew by the window on the all-terrain vehicle.

"They have too much testosterone for their own good," she sighed.

"That's not what you said last night," I teased.

She giggled. "I bet you didn't either."

10

AMISON

I STOPPED the truck in front of the main house, but didn't turn off the engine. The windows were open because the early evening was a perfect temperature. I hated wasting the good weather on my truck's AC. Before too long, it would be snowing again. The weather in Montana was fickle enough.

"Will you stay with me at my cabin?"

"You're asking?" Kitten asked, glancing up at me through those long, pale lashes.

Boone had been none too happy when we left, but he started his shift in the ER at seven, so he needed a solid night sleep, not a temptation like our Kitten in his bed.

There was no way he'd get any sleep if she were. Just like the night before. We'd barely slept.

Because of it, I was exhausted, yet my cock was hard again. No, still. Just thinking about what we'd done, how she'd felt, tasted, screamed, clenched, begged...fucked.

I would never forget the look on her face when I filled her for the very first time.

"I am. We claimed you last night, Kitten. You're ours now. Mine and Boone's, but that doesn't mean we'll boss you around. If want to stay in the main house, then I'll respect that."

"But you won't like it."

I shook my head. "No, I won't. After what happened to Kady there, I don't like the idea of you being up there alone, even if the fuck—, the man's dead."

"Someone tried to kill her."

"That's right."

"But I stayed there the past few nights."

"But you weren't ours then."

Sutton had killed the fucker, a single, perfect shot to his heart. But that had only been after the intruder stumbled around in the dark trying to find Kady. We'd gotten there in time to save her, although she'd done a pretty good job of it herself, hiding out on the porch roof. Since then, I'd wondered if the asshole would have ever found her. It had been a moonless, dark night and she'd been tucked in a corner by one of the chimneys.

The thought of Kitten like that, huddling on the roof, petrified, made my dick shrink. I'd respect her decision, but that didn't mean I wouldn't stay there with her, rifle in my lap as I watched her sleep. I'd been a cop, was familiar with the underbelly of society. I'd seen shit I would never forget. And I wanted none of that to touch Kitten.

Her cell rang in her bag. She pulled it out, sighed. "It's my mother. This is the third time she's called today."

She didn't look happy about a call from her mom. I spoke to my parents twice a week because, well, I liked them. I loved them, too, of course, but I enjoyed talking to them, hearing about their lives. It was obvious this wasn't the relationship Kitten had with her mother. I hated that for her because she was missing out.

I lifted my chin. "Answer it."

"But—"

"She's not going to stop. And when I get you in bed later, neither will I."

Her mouth fell open and her cheeks turned a pretty shade of pink. I couldn't help but wink at her, enjoying this lingering innocence about her.

She took the call, put her cell to her ear.

"Hello, Mother."

I wanted to listen in on this call, not to eavesdrop, per se, but to witness the dynamic between mother and daughter. To see how Kitten was affected. From what she told us the night before, she didn't like Congresswoman Vandervelk very much. I only knew of the woman from her political career and I'd looked her up online, studied her platform, her stand on important issues. While I might not have voted for her, she had an impressive track record. In Congress. With her daughter? Not so much.

I could hear the woman's voice, but couldn't make out the words.

"Yes, I'm still in Montana. Yes, the outline is progressing."

She'd mentioned her dissertation outline that was due to her advisor. But based on the way her body was tense, she wasn't telling the truth because she had no intention of continuing on in the program. She didn't like lying to her mother, but had yet to tell the woman off. From what she'd said, the stakes were high.

If her family did cut her off, she wouldn't be alone. We'd meant every word of what we'd said the night before. We wanted forever with Kitten. Hell, we wouldn't have fucked her otherwise. Taken her without protection. And when we'd found out she was a virgin...*fuck*. Her pussy was broken in just for our dicks. Molded to fit us. No one else would know the hot, wet grip of it. See his cum slip from her, knowing he'd filled her to the brim. Most likely filled her with a baby. Fuck no. Only me and Boone.

"Borstar? Yes, I received emails from them. A phone call, too. Yes." There was a pause as she listened. "Yes, the job description is impressive. Salary, too. Yes. Why? Because I don't want to work for an oil and gas company."

I could hear her mother talking then, her voice louder. Kitten pulled the phone away from her ear, turned and looked at me and mouthed, "Sorry."

There was nothing more that I could do than wink. This was her battle to fight. While I wanted to rip the phone out of her hand and tell her mother off, that wasn't going to end this shit.

I'd be here for her, Boone too, in any way she needed, but she had to come to the decision on her own to cut the ties. To walk away. To live her life the way she wanted. Last night, with us, was the first step. We'd take the next one, and the one after that, together.

"Mother, I have to go. No, I won't call the company back. I'm not interested. Good bye, Mother."

Her mother's muted voice continued to rant until Kitten ended the call.

She propped her head back, closed her eyes. "Sorry about that."

"You can't change your mother."

She turned her head, looked at me. Smiled. "I can change my father though."

"Very true. And see what that's done. You're here in Montana, claimed by two men and you've just told your mother you turned down the job offers. I'd say that's a good start."

"And your mom? Is she a power-grubbing congresswoman?"

I ran my hand over the back of my neck. "My mom lives with my dad in a beach house in Alabama. They were snowbirds, retiring and leaving the cold of Montana in the winter, but then decided to stay year round. When I was growing up, her job was taking care of me and my three brothers. Now, her job is to stay sane while living with my father." I smiled, thinking of my parents' loving relationship. "My father likes to tag along to the grocery store, look at everything, talk to people. My mother likes to get what's on her list. Get in, get out. He drives her crazy. I'm waiting for the call when I'll have to bail her out of jail."

Kitten smiled at my story. "That's sounds nice.

Normal. Although any woman who had four boys should get a medal from Congress. Hmm, maybe I can get my mom to give her one."

I remained quiet for a moment, let her think about that. I couldn't imagine two mothers being polar opposites more than ours.

"You were offered a job?" I let that question bounce around the cabin of the truck, even though I knew the answer.

"I told you yesterday they'd been in touch. Emails from several places, but one company is more persistent than the others. I guess they really want me working there."

"That must feel good, knowing all your hard work has paid off."

She shrugged. "I don't want the job, turned it down. I'm glad I finished my degree, but I'm just not interested anymore. It's not what I want."

"Okay." I nodded, ending the conversation, at least for now. Nothing about it would change overnight. "So will you stay with me?"

She glanced at the house. "Yes, but I need to pack a bag. I need something besides this outfit."

I looked her over, but didn't see the jean skirt and shirt she'd put back on. I saw her pale skin, the curve of her wide hips, the soft swells of her full breasts as she sprawled across Boone's sheets. Every bare inch of her.

"Pack it all, Kitten. You'll be in my bed or Boone's until we decide where all of us should live together."

Her wide eyes met mine. "You...I mean, I thought... you want to live with me?"

"Don't go saying we just met."

She pinched her lips together.

"I thought we've been over that."

She reached out, took my hand, curled her fingers around mine. "We have. It's just...I'm not used to someone, or two someones, wanting me. I'm not used to it."

I tugged her hand, pulled her close for a kiss. "Get used to it. Fast. Like we said, we wouldn't have taken that sweet cherry of yours if we didn't mean forever."

She blushed as bright as a cherry, stared at a button on my shirt. "You've had women before."

This was a dangerous conversation and I had to tread carefully. I understood the difference between Kitten and the woman I'd been with in the past. I'd fucked for twenty years. But it had never been with Kitten. It had meant nothing. A quick release. But I had to make sure she understood that.

"Yes, I have," I admitted. "But I never once fucked without a condom. She may have had access to my dick, but never once did I give a woman my heart. Until you."

Her full lips parted. "Jamison," she whispered. "What we did wasn't making love. It was—"

"Wild?"

"Yes."

"Dirty?"

"Yes."

"Really fucking naughty."

She went cold then. Her expression went blank and she stiffened.

"What? What is it?" I asked, recognizing things had

just changed, that something was wrong. I glanced out the windows to see if she saw something.

"I...I don't like that word. Naughty. I haven't been bad."

Shit. *Shit.* It was a trigger for her. *Naughty.* Of course, it would be. She'd been trying to be loved by her family so desperately that she probably hadn't done anything wrong in her life just so they'd give her a scrap of praise. And yet she'd most likely been shamed instead. Sent to boarding school because she just hadn't been good enough. She wasn't like her step-brothers and step-sister and because of that she believed she'd done something wrong.

I groaned, wishing I could heal this wound of hers. "No, you haven't been bad. You've done nothing wrong. You were perfect. You'll always be perfect, even if we argue. Nothing will change how much both Boone and I want you. Never." I evened my voice, made it soft. Gentle. I tugged her close, kissed her gently, a brushing of lips. "You're such a good girl."

She sighed, her warm breath blending with mine.

"When we touch, it's not just lust. I'm passionate about you, just as you are for me. I want you, your body. My body wants yours. But my mind, my heart, wants you, too. All of you. I'm desperately passionate about *you.*"

She glanced at me and I saw she was thinking about my words. The flicker of hope, surprise.

"That's what makes this special."

She nodded. "Yes, I understand. I'm passionate about you both, too. For the first time, I know exactly what I want."

"That's right. And sex? It's how we show each other just how much." I grinned then, sliding my thumb across her cheek. "And we've just gotten started. We haven't done all the possible ways to fuck. Yet. Do you want to know what I want to do with you?"

"Yes," she breathed.

She was back with me. Aroused again. Interested. I knew to steer clear of that word and I'd be sure to tell Boone about it.

"I want to fill you with my dick nice and slow, missionary position so I can watch your eyes as I do, before I fill you up with my cum."

She gave me the barest of whimpers.

"I'll give you that," I murmured softly. "I'll give you whatever you want."

I saw her blush, her eyes flare.

"Oh, Kitten, you've got something in mind, don't you?"

She licked her lips, nodded.

I groaned.

"Good girl." I turned off the truck. "Let's get your things, then we'll go back to the cabin and you can show me."

I had a feeling being with Kitten was going to be one wild night. And Boone? He'd be missing out, but he'd have his turn soon enough. Kitten could have all the dick she wanted.

"No, now. Here." Her small hands pushed me back and dove for my belt buckle.

 AMISON

"HERE?"

"I'm not a virgin anymore."

I stilled her hands, but didn't move them away. I could feel the heat of them through my jeans and there was a chance I'd come right then and there. "You've got to be sore."

She shook her head, bit her lip as she tugged her hands free, took hold of the zipper.

"Careful, Kitten." Moving my hands away, I let her do what she wanted. But, I didn't need to see Boone in the ER because of a fucking zipper injury. I'd rather be balls deep inside my very eager woman.

Once the jeans were open, she stopped. "Um, I thought it would pop out."

I laughed, but it was partial groan. She eyed my groin as if she hadn't eaten and my dick was her first meal in a week. I lifted my hips, worked my jeans down enough so that I did pop out.

"Oh," she said, in breathy surprise.

"I'm big and it lays down my thigh," I told her.

She flicked her gaze to mine for a second, then right back down at my lap. "Can I...put my mouth on it?"

Pre-cum emerged from the tip, a drop of it slid down the flared head.

"Fuck, yes."

Undoing her seat belt, she tucked her legs beneath her so she knelt on her seat, leaned over the center console. I couldn't miss the way her sweet ass was up in the air, her jean skirt riding up. Reaching out, I put my hand on the back of her silky thigh, slid it up to find her bare. No panties. I closed my eyes, pressed my head into the rest, knew that little scrap of silk was still in my shirt pocket.

Her tongue flicked out and I watched as she licked up the slide of pre-cum, licked her lips. The sight of her glancing up at me from my lap had another stream of it seeping out. "Don't tease, Kitten."

She smiled, like the Kitten who'd gotten the cream. Perhaps she was. But I wanted her to have all of it.

"Take me into that virgin mouth of yours. Show me what you can do."

She did as instructed, opening nice and wide and taking the entire head into that wet heat, her tongue swirling over it as if she were eating a fucking ice cream cone.

I groaned, watching her take me. It was the most erotic sight I'd ever seen.

"Grip the base. Good girl, yes like that. Now take it as deep as you can."

She quickly discovered her gag reflex and backed off. I wasn't the kind of fucker who forced a woman to swallow a dick. Just the tight suction as she drew her cheeks in, worked me with an eagerness I found endearing and hot as fuck, was enough for my balls to draw up.

I slid my hand up and cupped her pussy from behind. She moaned and the vibrations of it around my dick made me groan. "Jesus, Kitten. You're wet." I slipped a finger carefully inside. "And I can feel our cum nice and deep."

The idea that she was still full, that the proof that we'd been at her all night—and Boone this morning— made me feel so fucking possessive. She moaned again because I'd found the little ridge of her G-spot and curled my finger over it and I felt the vibrations clear to my balls. Her arousal made her wild. Voracious. She swirled her tongue over the very tip, lapping up the next batch of pre-cum I just spurted into her mouth.

"That's it. I can't take any more of those sweet lips." I grabbed her shoulders, carefully lifted her off of me. Her eyes were blurry as she looked to me.

"Why'd you stop? Don't you want to come in my mouth?"

With one hand, I pushed the button on my seat for

the back to recline. The other brushed over her bottom lip. "Fuck yes. But all our cum goes in that pussy."

Once the seat was flat, I scooped her up and onto my lap, her knees going to either side of my hips, which bunched her skirt about her waist. I pushed back so she had more room to maneuver with the steering wheel behind her.

Thank fuck she was tiny and she fit. She didn't even bump her head.

My cock rose up between us and she stared down at it, saw it slick from her mouth.

"It's all yours, Kitten."

She met my gaze and she bit her lip, shifting her hips. Then she tucked her hair behind her ears, glanced out the window, as if she'd just now realized we were in my truck and if someone drove up, we'd be seen. I didn't give a fuck. Of course, I was possessive of Kitten, but there would be no question that she was getting well-fucked, well-pleasured by one of her men and that while she was absolutely gorgeous when she came, all they could be was fucking jealous.

Kitten was *mine.*

I clenched my fists to keep from lifting her up and sinking her right onto my dick to prove that. Thank fuck she went up onto her knees so she hovered over me, then shimmied and slid, shifted her hips and worked herself down.

I had my eyes fixed right on her pussy and how my dick was disappearing inside. She was hot and so fucking tight. While I had no doubt she'd be wet all on her own, having our cum inside her already helped ease my way, especially since she had to be sore. We hadn't been rough with her, but an unused pussy needed some TLC and this wasn't it. Later, when I got her to my bed, I'd be sure to get my mouth on it to make it all better.

PENNY

ONE HAND GRIPPED the top of the passenger seat, the other in the open window, balancing myself as I rode Jamison like a cowgirl. I even had my boots on. Last night in the back of Boone's truck, Jamison had said I'd take their dicks for a ride. I didn't think he meant like this with all the world to possibly see. Maybe not the whole world, just the ranch hands. Maybe Mrs. Potts, the housekeeper.

I was just too eager to wait. Why should I? Jamison had all but promised me a wild night, and they'd definitely made good on it, but they'd made me insatiable. Needy. Greedy for cock.

A whole bunch of man-induced—no, *men*-induced— orgasms could short-circuit a woman's brain.

He didn't laugh. Nope. He just moved his hands out of the way and let me open his pants, then take him into my mouth. I'd felt powerful, knowing I made him hard, made the tip weep. Made him lose control. Me. Virginal me.

And I was like this because Jamison was right. I was passionate about him. About Boone, too. They were something I wanted with all my heart and that made all the difference. They made me realize I'd just been going through the motions of life until now. And finally, I knew what I wanted and I was going to take it. And that was Jamison's dick. I wanted it. Wanted to share this overflowing passion with him. I needed this connection, this bond.

And it wasn't *naughty*. I wasn't naughty taking what I wanted because it was...right.

I'd made him crazy enough to tug me over the center console and onto his lap. Through gritted teeth, he told me to have my way with him. With a gorgeous cowboy, all muscles and strong hands. Powerful thighs, thick cock. This man who could overpower me, hurt me, destroy me, lay in wait for me to take what I wanted from him.

And so I was taking full advantage of that welcome.

When I first lowered myself, I felt the burn, the soreness of being filled again, wiggling my hips to take him in. But it quickly, no, immediately was replaced by pleasure. Somehow, Jamison was hitting every hot spot I had, and I was on the brink of coming.

I'd been close before, the two of them leaving me simmering all day with their touches, their words, their darned promises of what they were going to do to me that I'd mentally said fuck it and jumped Jamison.

I laughed, let my head fall back as I reveled in the thick feel of Jamison deep inside me, how I could take from him what I wanted. Being with him, to some, might be considered stifling. Him and Boone, both, were dominant men. But it was the opposite, I felt. I felt free for once in my life. They accepted me as I was, wanted me, and based on the way their cocks were always hard, wanted me. Jamison was giving me the room, in this moment, to explore my own desires, learn from them. Even *use* him.

I clenched around him, felt the flare of heat, the sweat bloom on my skin from that simple motion. He was *really* deep. This angle had him bumping the top of me and I knew I took him all—especially when I was sitting on top of his thighs. His hands tightened on my hips, but he did nothing to move me.

"Kitten," he warned, the sound gravelly. His gray eyes held mine, a hint of warning there. For what, I didn't know.

I grinned slyly. "What?"

His hands came up then, not to get me to move, but to grab the front of my shirt, rip it open. The buttons were no match for his strength and they went flying. His eyes flared at the sight of my breasts in the lacy bra.

"Ride me. I want to watch those gorgeous breasts bounce as you make yourself come all over my dick."

I felt myself get wet at his dirty talk and decided to take mercy on him, on both of us, and began to move. Up, down, swirl my hips. Over and over until I sensed I was close, rode him toward the pleasure, taking him faster and faster. My thighs would be sore later from the workout, but that was so...later.

"Jamison. God, I'm going to...oh, yes. It's so good."

I was so lost to the need to come that I missed that his hands had moved. One finger pressed against my back entrance in a slippery circle. His other hand cupped my breast and pinched a hard nipple through my bra.

"Jamison!" My eyes flew open and I met his narrowed

gaze. Saw the way his jaw was clenched, his cheeks flushed.

"Like that?"

Did I? I had no idea there were so many nerve endings...there, that it would feel. So. Good.

"Fuck yes," I cried. I couldn't help but squeeze and clench around him, my mind giving up the fight and my body taking over.

He pulled away, gripped my hips and lifted me off of him.

"Wha—"

"Turn around."

I worked my legs over his waist, difficult in the small space, until I straddled him again facing away from him. As if I were driving the truck. My hands went to the steering wheel. Jamison slipped his thumb over my pussy, dipped it inside before pulling it free and working me down onto his cock. This direction had him hitting all different places inside. I whimpered, glad to have him back inside.

"You came with my finger pressing against your ass. Time for more."

His palm flattened at the very base of my spine right before his slick thumb pressed to my back entrance and slipped in. Between the angle and the lubrication, he went right in.

I groaned at the stretch, the slight burn.

"Feel full?" he asked, his voice rough.

I nodded, glanced over my shoulder at him.

"Fuck me, Kitten. Fuck the cum right out of me and

you'll see what it will be like when we both get in you, one of us in your ass, the other in your pussy."

I could picture it, me being between both of my lovers. The idea of it wasn't scary. No, the feel of Jamison's thick finger proved I liked butt stuff. And when I began to move, lifting and lowering myself as I used the steering wheel for balance and leverage, he slid his thumb carefully in and out. Not too far, but enough to let me know an actual dick would be...incredible.

It was too much. All of it. The first orgasm had primed me for more, making me so sensitive that it wasn't hard to tip over the edge. And his thumb...

"Come for me. Come now."

It may have been the gravelly bite of his words, the surprising pleasure/pain of his fingers, or because I felt him swell even thicker inside me, but I came. I screamed, the sound, I knew, carried out the open windows and across the open ranch land.

"That's it. Milk the cum from my balls. Yes. Fuck. You love something in your ass. My dick will be there soon. Ah, you're going to love it."

My hair was long down my back, my breathing ragged as I used Jamison for my pleasure, eked out every bit of it as I worked my pussy on his cock, rubbed my clit against his body as he continued to talk filthy.

I wanted everything he said. Every. Single. Word.

His thumb pressed even deeper as his entire body went taut. A deep groan escaped his lips as he came. I glanced over my shoulder then, watched him as he did so, seeing him lost to the world, to the pleasure he'd pulled from my body. At the same time, I could feel the hot cum spurt inside me. So deep. So much of it that I would be marked, inside and out, for days. He shifted his hips, up and down, the tiniest amount as he came, his cum starting to escape around him, coating my thighs, his lap.

I couldn't catch my breath, couldn't do anything but hold on tight.

Eventually, his hands moved away, I lifted myself off him, turned back around so I faced him once more.

"Wait," he said, his voice soft now, tender, as he looked at my pussy, hovering over him.

His dick was glistening, coated in our combined fluids. Still hard. Angry looking, as if he still had to come.

"What?" I asked.

"I love seeing you coated in my cum."

His hand cupped me, gently, and began to work all that cum that slipped out over every inch of my pussy, even working some of it back up into me.

"Get my cell."

It was in the center console and I picked it up. "You're not taking a picture."

"Fuck no. Find Boone's number. Call him."

I wasn't sure why, but I nodded and did as he wanted. Boone answered on the first ring.

"Hi, Boone," I said, my voice deep and rough, probably from screaming.

"Put it on speaker," Jamison said.

I pushed the button.

"Hi, Kitten," Boone replied.

"Tell him what we just did, that I fucked your broken in pussy with his cum easing the way. That you came hard because I had a thumb working that virgin ass. In my truck."

I heard Boone's groan through the phone.

"Kitten?" he asked.

I cleared my throat, repeated Jamison's words.

"You just got me so hard," Boone told me when I was done. "Want to know what I'm going to do to you tomorrow night when I pick you up?"

I bit my lip, looked at Jamison. Knew it was going to make me all hot again. I wouldn't be able to wait until then to come again. I'd need Jamison to ease the ache later. And I knew he would. Knew his dick would be up to the task.

Jamison's hand came up, stroked over my hair, down my arm. An easy, light gesture. A tender one that was completely at odds with the wild fucking we'd just completed.

"Tell him, Kitten. Tell Boone exactly what you want, no matter how dirty it is. He'll give it to you. You'll get more than a finger in that tight ass. He'd get a plug in you, and soon one of our dicks. We'll take that virginity, too. You're ours. Always."

Yes, I was seeing that now. Kady had been right. They wanted more. They wanted it all and I felt good. Not just my pussy, but my heart, too.

I put my hand on Jamison's chest, nodded. "Yes, Boone. Tell me. I can't wait."

12

OONE

IT HAD BEEN a week since we claimed Kitten for the first time and while she'd spent each night at either my house or Jamison's cabin, we were in the main house for a large group dinner. The space was the easiest for such a task, the kitchen large, the dining room table big enough to fit a bunch of oversized men.

She'd insisted on cooking for everyone, all the ranch hands plus Kady and her men. Both women decided a weekly meal together was good for all of us. Since I was pussy-whipped, or *Kitten-whipped,* if she wanted to cook for our pseudo big family, I'd eat. Happily.

Other than this meal, the house went neglected. Kady lived with her men and Kitten had spent every night since we claimed her in one of our beds. I didn't want her staying here. Jamison *really* didn't want it. He was adamant about it since he'd been there when the fucker went after Kady. Seen the dead body, the knife he'd had on him. It would remain vacant, except for some of these big group get-togethers, until the next Steele daughter was found and moved in. Before then, Jamison and Riley were working with a security company to get it well protected.

Jamison had read Patrick and Shamus the fucking riot act for not watching out for Kitten at the Silky Spur. Based on the way they were all but falling over themselves for her and Kady, they'd gotten the message loud and clear.

Since then, they'd been on their best behavior, which was why they popped up, their chairs scraping across the wood floor in their haste, when Jamison said, "You know what the rule is," Jamison told the table at large. He stood and grabbed his plate, winked at Kitten. "He who cooks, doesn't clean."

They grabbed as many empty dishes as possible and beelined right for the kitchen on Jamison's heels.

Sutton, one of the other hands, remained in his seat, arms crossed, slowly shaking his head. He was older than the others, close to my age and had spent years in the military. He was ruthless enough to shoot the fucker that had gone after Kady. A perfect, single shot right through the heart. If he'd been at the Silky Spur last week, no way would he have let Kitten out of his sight.

Riley stood, leaned down and kissed the top of Kady's head, murmured in her ear, "I'll get the dessert. I'm looking forward to the whipped cream." Her face turned beet red and she refused to look up from her plate. I had to wonder what the three of them had done with the sweet topping.

"Everything was delicious, Penny," Sutton said, placing his napkin on the table.

She'd gone simple with hamburgers and all the fixings, potato wedges and a salad. Brownies—with whipped cream. And she'd been smart enough to know big men ate big quantities and had made tons.

Beneath the table, I took hold of Kitten's hand, squeezed it. She blushed, pleased by the praise. She'd been soaking it up all week, relaxing and settling into her life in Barlow. Out from under her mother's ruthless dictates, she was blossoming. The congresswoman had called a few times, but Kitten had let them all go to voicemail. While I would never lay a hand on a woman, I wanted to with Nancy Vandervelk. She'd used her daughter's need for motherly affection as a weapon. If Kitten toed the line, did exactly what her mother wanted, she was given scraps of attention. Affection. If she didn't... Kitten knew what would happen and hadn't been prepared for the consequences. That was why she was twenty-two and had just finished a Master's program in an area where she had no interest.

No longer. I had to agree with Kitten. Aiden Steele had saved her. His death had brought out the truth of her past. No, it had pulled out all of her mother's lies. Knowing this allowed Kitten to understand more about herself and begin to break away. The fuck-all was, her mother had made her feel like the real Penelope Vandervelk was a failure for wanting something different than her mother. To be different than her overly ambitious step-brothers and step-sister. But she was only a Vandervelk on paper. Her personality, her spirit, was all Steele.

She hadn't confronted her mother yet, but it was only a matter of time. When she truly believed Jamison and I were around for good, for forever, she'd have the confidence, the support in place to finish the job.

How she didn't completely trust yet only proved how many wounds her mother had inflicted. She gave herself to us wholeheartedly, but until she resolved things with her mother, she'd never be completely free. Because of that, she'd moved from house to house, Jamison's and mine, depending on whether I was working. Soon we'd work out where we could all live together. One house for the three of us. And all the kids that she was going to give us. She'd get the real family she wanted so badly. That I wanted to give her.

She'd shared so much of herself in the past seven days—she was allergic to blueberries, loved action-adventure movies, liked the color purple based on the sheer quantity of sexy lavender lingerie she taunted us with, and was as ravenous for us as we were for her. The only casualty were the sexy panties we ripped off her.

She was far from a virgin now. That first night, she'd been right about us. We'd been thinking she'd be all tentative and fearful of two big men and even bigger dicks wanting to get in her, all the dark and dirty things we wanted to do to her just because she'd never fucked before.

She'd told us off, stomped that cute little cowboy boot

and had never looked back. I smiled to myself thinking about that, that the only time she *did* look back was when I had her in my bed and took her from behind and she told me deeper. Harder. More.

I shifted in my seat, my dick hard, just thinking about how she'd pushed back, giving as much as she got until we came together in a hot, sweaty mess.

As for the rest? Kitten was here with us and that alone allowed me to be patient. Patient for her to be ready for more, for the next step. A ring on her finger. That would probably happen in the next week or so, when she most likely missed her period. I'd done a rotation in OB/GYN during my residency, knew all about the best days to get pregnant. For Kitten, until I knew about her cycle, I couldn't actually calculate the days she'd be ovulating, but was pretty sure we'd hit every one of them, fucking her and filling her up sometimes twice a day. She was young, healthy. I had no doubt we'd bred her.

When I groaned, low in my chest, she turned to look at me, a little frown in her brow. Taking the hand I held, I moved it to my lap, settled it on my dick. Her eyes flared wide.

As soon as we knew for sure, we'd be hightailing it to the courthouse to make it official. While she couldn't legally marry both of us, she'd have the protection my name provided. He and I had talked about it and legally, she'd be mine. But that didn't mean she'd be his any less. She knew she was both of ours. The mixed cum on her thighs was proof. That baby would know not just one dad, but two. Know the love Kitten never had. Until now.

Kitten cupped my dick, gave it a slight squeeze.

I stood, tugged on her hand and lifted her out of the chair. "We'll be right back."

As I led her out of the room and down the hall to Aiden Steele's office, I heard a few chuckles, but I didn't pay them any mind. As soon as I closed the door to the masculine room, I undid my belt buckle.

"You want my dick, Kitten?"

She looked up at me with very precocious eyes. When she licked her lips, her pink tongue flicking out, I knew we no longer had a sexual innocent. She was now a vixen who knew just how to get what she wanted.

"Oh yes," she all but purred. "The plug you put in me is driving me crazy."

Before she'd left Jamison's cabin, I'd worked the smallest plug into her. She'd taken bigger over the past week, but I'd wanted this one to stay in over the meal, so she'd remember who she belonged to. To have in the back of her mind that one day soon we'd claim her together. For me, it was hot as fuck knowing she had it in her all that time.

She started to fall to her knees before me, but I caught her by the arm. I slowly shook my head, kept her from kneeling and taking me in her mouth. "You know the rule. Ladies first."

"But we have to be quick. I don't want anyone to know what we're doing."

I walked her backwards toward the wall. "Kitten, *everyone* knows what we're doing. And as for fast—"

"Oh!" she gasped when I lifted her up, cupped her glorious ass in my palms until she wrapped her legs around my waist.

"—I'll have you coming all over me in about thirty seconds."

She was so small, so light, that I leaned in and pinned her in place as I pulled myself free.

"Still bare beneath this pretty dress?"

Nodding, she bit her lip and rested her head back against the wood paneling.

"Still like the plug?"

She nodded again, her cheeks flushing a pretty pink.

When I found her slick heat, slid over the plush folds she thought were too big, I groaned and pre-cum seeped from me. She had me primed and ready to fuck at all times. And the feel of her, all swollen and ready for me, was too much. My finger bumped the base of the plug. I couldn't wait.

Lowering her, she slid right down onto my dick. She gasped out and I leaned in, kissed her neck. "Shh, Kitten. Don't let anyone hear your little cries."

I pulled my hips back, plunged deep.

"More?" I said, breathing in her soft scent.

"More," she whispered.

I didn't hold back then. Jamison and I had trained her to come all over our cocks, her pussy responding to us beautifully. I knew her body, knew the spots inside I had to stroke that would set her off. And I aimed for them, rubbed over them until she came. I felt her begin to milk me, pull me in, try to hold me as deep as possible, as if her body craved my cum. She had her lips pinched closed as her cheeks flushed, her moans stifled.

"That's my good girl." Jamison had told me about her trigger word, that it shamed her to be considered naughty, even if she were anything but. Instead, we praised her often, ensuring she knew she was absolutely perfect.

I thrust deep two more times and followed her over, filling her right up. Load after load of cum until she'd drained me dry. Until my brain was fried and I could do nothing but cup her ass with one hand, press against the wall with the other.

She couldn't get down on her own. I was too tall and she was impaled on my dick. Little aftershocks rippled along her pussy and I was ready to go again.

But Kitten was right. A quickie was all fine and good. Everyone understood the need behind one of those, but anything longer was bad form.

I bent my knees, finally set her on her feet, my cock slipping free. With the hem of her dress still caught up at her waist, I couldn't miss the hot gush of cum that slipped down her thigh.

"I don't think that was thirty seconds," she said.

Nope. I grinned, feeling very virile. "Tonight, when Jamison and I get you between us, I promise we'll go a lot longer. All night, if we don't fuck you unconscious."

She grinned at that. "Promises, promises," she replied, using the same words she'd uttered the night we'd first taken her. She slipped out the door and down the hall to the powder room before I could reply. *Vixen.*

I righted my pants, then returned to the dining room.

13

OONE

JAMISON WAS IN HIS SEAT, the table empty of everything from the meal, Sutton leaning forward with his elbows on the table. I heard the sound of washing dishes coming from the kitchen. Cord had moved to a seat closer to the other men, Kady on his lap.

Jamison gave me a once over and only the slight turn of his lip indicated he knew what I'd been up to with Kitten. "Sutton was telling us about a man who came to the ranch yesterday."

I stilled as I pulled out my chair. "Oh?"

Sutton glanced up at me. Nodded. He had close-cropped brown hair, and I could see the crease in it from his hat. His eyes were dark, intense. He was quiet and calm like Jamison, but he had a sharp edge to him, as if he'd seen things, lived through hardships or horrors that changed him. And that kept him quiet. So when he spoke, Jamison listened. Hell, we all did.

"Said he was a surveyor."

Riley came back in through the door with a platter of brownies in his hands and a can of the spray whipped cream tucked under his arm.

"Know anything about a surveyor?" Jamison asked him.

He put the platter down in the center of the table, tossed the whipped cream to Cord who caught it easily one handed.

"No."

"He shared his ID and I wrote the info down. He's a small fish in the big oil pond."

Shit. This wasn't good.

Jamison's eyebrows went up and he met my gaze as he responded. "Big oil? Which company?"

"Borstar. Ever heard of it?"

I shook my head as Jamison said, "Actually, yes."

I frowned.

"Last week," he explained. "Penny mentioned being offered a job with them. You were working." The last, he said to me.

"A job offer with whom?" Kitten asked.

I turned at her return, looked her over. So fucking gorgeous. Her cheeks were a little flushed, but otherwise there was no outward sign that she'd just been fucked. Her casual dress was a pale blue and matched her eyes. Not that it was immodest; the cut of it was like a t-shirt, but fell to her knees. And was perfect for easy access.

Now I knew why Cord and Riley loved Kady in dresses so much.

Jamison held out his arm and Kitten went over to him and he wrapped it about her waist. Her being so small, they were almost the same height with him seated.

"When you talked with your mother last week, you mentioned Borstar," he said, his voice soft and gentle in the way he only had for her.

"That's right. I had job offers from Borstar and two others." She bit her lip. "A small company in Iceland and the last wasn't an oil company, but does soil clean-up that contracts solely for Super Fund sites."

I'd heard about places that were classified as Super Funds, like the town of Shelby a few hours north of Barlow, and how the government was required to mitigate environmental damage. As for Iceland, I knew little. I'd never even heard of Borstar.

"Sutton met a man from Borstar who showed up on your land," Jamison added.

Your land. It did belong to her, and Kady, and the three other mystery sisters.

Kitten looked to Sutton. "A surveyor," he repeated.

"He'd be looking at topography, geographical specifications like rivers or a creek. Large rock formations, outcroppings, buttes." She frowned, considered, then glanced at Kady. "You didn't ask for one?"

"Me?" Kady's eyes widened in surprise, then she laughed. "I'm an east coast girl and wouldn't know a butte from my butt. I've barely figured out how to ride a horse."

Jamison chuckled, stroked his knuckles down Kitten's

cheek. "That's true, about the horse part, but she's getting much better at riding." He softened his teasing with a wink.

I saw Kitten's cheeks heat as she glanced at the floor.

"Then what was he doing here? Looking for oil?" I asked. "Can someone just look at land and know there's oil on it?"

I wasn't involved with Steele ranch. While I was born and raised in Barlow and considered myself a little bit of a cowboy, I was also a city slicker. A doctor. I spent my days in the ER dealing with everything from the flu to alcohol poisoning to cardiac arrest. A completely different experience than riding the range on the back of a horse. Even though I was friends with Jamison, I didn't come to the ranch often, maybe a few times a year if one of the guys were sick. Eight years I'd been away, at college and then hospitals from Chicago to Austin for my residency and other years training to be a doctor.

"It's possible to find patches of oil that have seeped to the surface. Unlikely, but scientifically possible," Kitten said. "But you can study rocks, see if there's a presence of hydrocarbons."

She stopped there, looked around. While none of us had glazed looks on our faces, she was definitely talking over our heads. She recognized that and looked to Sutton. "Did he have any equipment with him? Something to collect rocks or soil samples. Maybe a machine that looks like a fancy-looking metal detector?"

Sutton shook his head. "He had a small backpack, nothing bigger than what a kid would take to school, water bottle in the side pocket. He had his phone out, so maybe he was taking some pictures?"

"A company that wants you to work for them has a surveyor stop by your property," I said aloud. This wasn't over. Sutton may have driven the man off, but it wasn't over. I could feel it.

"Maybe our father made arrangements with them before he died?" Kady wondered aloud.

"It's possible, sweetness, but we didn't find any record of it when we cleaned out his office, his papers," Riley told her. "There's no mention anywhere of any kind of oil or mineral rights leasing. As far as I know, the land's untouched. If Borstar made a deal with your daddy, they'd be in touch with me about any dividend checks since I'm executor. Those you can't hide or avoid the taxes on."

"True," Kady finished, shrugging her shoulders.

An old arrangement with Steele was a plausible scenario, but Riley was right. He'd have gotten a letter from the IRS if there were any unpaid taxes.

I took hold of Kitten's chin, had her look at me. "I think you should reach out to your contact there, see what's going on."

Kitten met my gaze. She had her bottom lip between her teeth, a sure sign her smart mind was at work and thinking about more than just hydrocarbons. "All right. Do you think we're in danger?" she asked, glancing at Kady.

The women had had several girls-only get-togethers since they first met at my house. No doubt Kady had shared what had happened to her.

Cord had Kady tucked on his lap, an arm about her waist. While I saw the hard glint in his eyes at the possibility, there was no way he was letting anything happen to her. No fucking chance.

"While he seemed harmless enough, the guy's a credible threat. I'll call Archer," Sutton said, getting to his feet.

Archer was the town's sheriff. He'd been involved with Kady's murder-for-hire case and knew to take this seriously. While Jamison and I had gone to high school around the same time with him, he was close with Sutton. If they ever found a woman, they'd definitely share her. Someday.

"I'll also update the men, tell them to keep an eye out," Sutton added. After the fuck-up at the Silky Spur, they'd be watching. "I'll keep you posted on what Archer says."

Strange men on Steele Ranch land was not a good thing, especially when the women seemed to be directly involved. It couldn't just be coincidence that Kitten inherited and Borstar followed.

He gave the women a nod, then strode into the kitchen where the dishes were still being washed, letting the door swing back and forth behind him.

"Borstar is based in Texas, I think," Kitten said. "Their offices are closed this time of night. I'll contact the HR person tomorrow."

"Tomorrow." Jamison stood, lifting Kitten over his shoulder as he did so, and grabbed the whipped cream off the table in front of Cord. "I'm taking this. Thanks for the idea."

Kitten's calls to be put down were ignored as Jamison strode from the room. He didn't close the front door behind him, knowing I would follow. I looked to the others, who were grinning. Sutton would connect with Archer and the men would be vigilant. Kady was safe with her men and Kitten would be safest with us. Especially between us. That didn't mean she wouldn't worry and that was why Jamison had carried her off. He wanted her distracted and knew just how to do it. I couldn't agree with him more, especially since the quickie had done nothing to ease the ache in my balls. They were heavy and full of cum for her already.

I shrugged, then followed, my hard dick leading the way.

14

ENNY

"WHAT IS THIS PLACE?" I asked, putting my hand on the back of the passenger seat, looking out the front windshield. Jamison turned off his truck.

After eating at the diner in town for a late breakfast, we'd driven out of town, the opposite direction of Steele Ranch. He'd turned off the main road five minutes ago, followed a dirt road for another few, before turning into a short driveway.

We were closer to the mountains here, the setting lush and green. A river was to our right, the water flowing high and hard from the runoff coming down through the canyon. Directly before us was a house. An old, two-story farmhouse. Crisp clapboard siding, a front porch with a swing, a steep metal roof. It was reminiscent of the house in the American Gothic painting, only larger. Based on the size, I estimated it to have at least four bedrooms. Yet it was quaint and charming. Even from the truck, it had a welcoming, lived-in feel to it. In the distance, I could see another house, so it wasn't as isolated as Steele Ranch.

"This is where I grew up."

"Your parents' house?"

"That's right," Jamison said, taking off his seatbelt and getting out of the truck.

By the time I got mine off, he had my door open to help me down. He took my hand and led me toward the house, Boone following right behind.

"I thought they moved to Alabama."

"They did. I bought it from them." I stumbled at the words and Jamison stopped, looked down at me. His hat cast his face in shadow. "What?"

"You have this beautiful house and yet you live at Steele Ranch. Why don't you live here?"

He shrugged. "I've been waiting for you."

He started walking again and I followed along. *He'd been waiting for me?*

"You didn't even know about me a month ago. How could you have been waiting?"

Unlocking the front door, he pushed it open, waited for me to enter first. The floors were wood, the walls a soft cream. Directly before me was a stairwell with a banister perfect for sliding down. A formal living room was on the left, a central hallway that led to the back of the house in the middle and a dining room to the right. There was some furniture, a couch and a large bookshelf, a sideboard. Curtains hung at the windows. The floors were bare. It seemed Jamison's parents had chosen to leave some pieces behind.

With all the windows closed, the house was warm, the air a touch stale, but the interior was spotless. It appeared as if the owners were away for the weekend instead of living elsewhere.

"This house is meant for a family," Jamison told me, taking off his hat and hanging it on the newel post, as if he'd done it a hundred—a thousand—times before. "A big one."

"One we want to have with you," Boone added.

I spun on my heel, looked up at him. Unlike Jamison, he never wore a hat. His hair was so dark, almost black and I knew exactly how it felt between my fingers. He'd shaved this morning, but the hint of his whiskers would appear in a few hours. He wore jeans and a t-shirt with the name of his medical school on the front. Casual, laid back. Yet his look was anything but.

He was serious. His *words* were serious.

"You want us to...what? Live here?"

He nodded.

"What about your house?" I glanced over my shoulder at Jamison. "Or your cabin at Steele Ranch?"

"That cabin's for a bachelor. It's too small for a family," he said. "I've lived there because it's easy."

"We can live in my house if you want. Hell, we can build a house on Steele Ranch land if you want, but this place...I grew up coming here. Loved it. The noise, the chaos. Something was always in the slow cooker and the house always smelled so good. Like pot roast."

I didn't say anything, just glanced between them.

They wanted to live here. In this house. It was tangible—and blatant—proof of the forever they wanted to have with me.

"What's going on in that gorgeous brain of yours?" Boone asked.

"I believed you," I said on a big exhale. "I did. But this...it's real. You're serious."

Jamison huffed. "Kitten, I should sit on the steps and take you over my knee. What do you think we've been doing with you?"

"Well, um...getting to know each other?" I replied.

"You were going to say fucking," Boone countered, crossing his arms over his chest.

I shook my head. "No. It's more than that."

"That's right," Jamison said moving to lean against the wall. I recognized his casual stance, but it was anything but. When he was bothered by something, he grew quieter, not louder. "It's more than fucking. It's loving. We've been loving you."

Blood drained from my head and I had to sit down. *Loving.* On shaky legs, I moved to the steps, sat down on one of the worn pine treads. I had to imagine how many times Jamison and his brothers had flown down these steps to get some of that pot roast.

"You never said—"

"What?" Boone asked, walking over and squatting down before me so we were at eye level. "That we loved you?"

I nodded. Tears burned the back of my eyes and I blinked them away, yet Boone still blurred before me.

"We told you with every touch, every hug. Kiss. With everything we are."

The tears fell then, hot, down my cheeks. When I wiped them away, blinked, Boone held something before me.

A ring.

"Oh my god."

"We can go to the courthouse, make this all legal, but it won't make a difference. Not to me."

Jamison pushed off the wall, moved to the steps, sat beside me so our sides touched.

"A piece of paper doesn't mean anything." Jamison turned, put his hand on my chest so his pinkie rested on the swell of my breast. His touch was reverent, not sexual. "It's what's in here that matters."

Jamison reached into his shirt pocket, pulled out a ring of his own. Both were simple bands, nothing fancy. Jamison's was gold, Boone's platinum.

"Marry us, Kitten. Be our wife. To have and to hold and everything else," Boone said.

"Babies. Lots of them."

"And pot roasts."

"Lots of them," Jamison added and I couldn't help but laugh.

The tears were still falling now, but joy filled my heart. I'd never felt so happy, so whole. So...complete.

"I...I love you. Both of you."

I'd never said the words before. There hadn't been anyone who I'd felt enough for to have earned those words. Who deserved them. I *thought* I loved my mother. I'd ached for her acceptance, her approval, for my entire life. I'd craved love from her. But since I'd never received it from her, not once had I ever felt that she loved me, and I never had it for her in return.

But what Boone said was right. They hadn't said the words, but they'd shown me their love. In everything they did, in every look, touch. Breath.

"Those are the words I've longed to hear. Hoped for. I've waited for you, the woman we'd share, love and grow old with, for thirty-eight years," Jamison said. "I love you, too."

"Ah, Kitten, I love you, too," Boone added. "Marry us."

I nodded, my throat clogged with tears. They waited, as usual, with their never-ending patience for me to pull myself together. "Yes. God, yes, I'll marry you."

"We claimed you that first night and you have been ours since then. When we took your virginity, we told you forever then and meant it when we filled you with our cum, with our baby." Boone slid his finger on my ring finger.

I didn't know I was pregnant. Not for sure. But he believed we'd made a baby. With all the love between us, I had no doubt it was possible. I felt no different, but we'd know in a few days.

Jamison took hold of my hand, slipped his ring on so the two were side by side. Proof that I belonged to both of them.

"You're ours, Kitten," Jamison said, his tone vehement. He took hold of my chin, kissed me.

It went on and on, hot and with lots of tongue. My hands found their way into his hair and I held on. He stood, scooped me up and carried me up the stairs, not once breaking the kiss. I had to wonder if I would always be carried off to the nearest bed. By the time he laid me down on a soft mattress, I had my legs wrapped around his waist, my ankles hooked at the back.

He lifted his head and I looked into his gray eyes. Saw the heat, even the smile there. I loved the way the corners crinkled, the way his look softened just for me. "When I was a teenager, I dreamed about fucking a woman in this bed."

The walls were a soft blue, the bed narrow. "This is your bedroom from growing up?"

"Yup," he replied, his gaze dropping to my mouth.

"You dreamed about fucking a woman in this bed, or did you dream in this bed about fucking?" I asked, trying to get clarification.

He stilled, frowned. "Definitely both."

He stood to his full height, Boone moving beside him. They loomed over me as I lay on my back. Big, virile men with very obvious bulges in their jeans. And those bulges were all for me. I knew what they felt like in my grip, what they felt like in my mouth, and deep inside my pussy.

"You're every man's fantasy, but you're ours," Boone said. "And it's time for us to claim you together."

I arched my back, clenched my pussy. "I know you just had me last night, but yes, I want more. I'm... insatiable with you two."

Boone leaned down, put his hand beside my head and kissed me. He kissed differently than Jamison. More insistent, intentional, but gentler somehow. He tasted different, too. I liked both of them, needed both of them to feel complete.

"This means you'll take both our cocks. I'll be in your ass, take that last virginity, while Jamison's fucking that sweet pussy."

I moaned at the thought. I loved ass play. Loved that they used their fingers, the plugs on me. God, having it in last night while we had the big group dinner had been so hot. It was like we were sharing this dark secret only the three of us knew about. It felt intimate. And the sensation? Exquisite. Turned out, it made me come. Hard. And to think of Boone's big cock deep inside me there...I squirmed.

"Yes, please. I want that so much."

He kissed me once more, his free hand going to the buttons on my shirt, getting them all undone and deftly opening the front clasp of my bra. His nose nudged the lace to the side and he had his mouth on my nipple, strongly pulling on it in the way he knew I liked. It was as if his action sent a direct message to my pussy to get all wet.

Jamison's cell rang and a second later, so did Boone's.

I watched as he clenched his jaw, closed his eyes for a moment.

"What?" Jamison growled, Boone's cell still ringing.

"Yes, she's with me. Boone, too." There was a pause. "Who? You're fucking kidding me."

Boone's eyes met mine before he pushed off to stand. His cell had stopped ringing, most likely whoever Jamison was speaking with knew we were all together.

I lay there, shirt opened, watching as Jamison glanced down at me even as he listened.

"We'll be there in thirty minutes."

He ended the call.

"What's the matter?" I asked.

"You've got a visitor at Steele Ranch."

I frowned. "Kady?"

Jamison slowly shook his head. "That was Sutton. A woman showed up at the ranch with a handful of men in stiff suits and sunglasses."

I popped up off the bed, my fingers flying to fix my bra and shirt. Nothing made me lose interest in being taken by both my men at the same time. But this did. "My mother. My mother is here."

15

AMISON

It's not often a guy's cock blocked by a member of Congress. I hoped it was the first, and last, time. As I drove down the Steele Ranch's long, dusty driveway, I flicked my gaze up to the rearview mirror, checking on Kitten. She'd been quiet, looking out the window the whole way. Her relationship with her mother had come to a head and I hoped this would be the showdown Boone and I had been waiting for.

A parent had to cut the fucking apron strings at some point, but because Nancy Vandervelk hadn't yet—the perfect example of a helicopter parent—she perhaps assumed she could maintain control over her adult daughter as well. Kitten had enabled her mother to do so. Until now.

Now, she had us. She had the power of the Steele name, even if it wasn't hers legally. She had the backing of Kady, Riley and Cord. The other men on the ranch. She had a family. Not a blood one, but a group of people who truly cared about her and her well-being.

And she had money. Money to live her life where she wanted, how she wanted. And when we took her to the courthouse to be legally wed, she'd take Boone's name. What she didn't know was that he was rich as fuck. He had Copper King money in his past. His Butte predecessors had made fortunes in the copper rush in the 1800s and generations after that were smart enough to invest the money, to make it grow. He knew what it was like to have woman after him for his money and he hid the wealth well. Kitten didn't give a shit about it. She hadn't from the start.

But he'd tested her that first night in the gas station, to see if she was more interested in a Jaguar in her garage than anything else. She'd passed, and claimed Boone's heart then and there.

She didn't need her mother in her life. If Nancy Vandervelk was going to be a stone cold bitch, then Kitten could just send her on her way.

I had a mother. So did Boone. Both of them were eager to hop on the next flight and meet our Kitten, hug her right up and never let go.

But this meeting, all of it, was up to Kitten. If she wasn't ready to deal with her mom, I'd be disappointed, but I'd be patient. Family was great, but they were hard on the emotions.

All that mattered was that Kitten was safe and happy. And that Nancy Vandervelk's job kept her two time zones away.

I parked to the side of the main house, two identical black SUVs were parked out front and I had no intention of blocking them in. If they wanted to leave, and take the Wicked Witch of the East with them, I wasn't going to stop them. Two suits stood on the front porch steps, the woman herself or the rest of her entourage not visible.

I glanced over my shoulder at Kitten.

"Ready?"

Boone unclipped his seatbelt, spun around. "We can leave. Jamison can turn his truck around and head right on out of here. She may have come all this way, but you don't have to see her."

She smiled at us. "Thank you for that. But she wouldn't have come here if it weren't important, at least to her. She won't linger."

But the fallout might.

"Trust me. She likes a lot of concrete." She opened her door, and we followed, flanked her as she walked around to the front of the house. "Let's get this over with."

———

PENNY

IT HAD BEEN sixteen days since I'd seen my mother last.

Yes, I knew the exact count. Since I was ten, I'd been parted from her more than I'd been with her, so it wasn't anything new. But I was. New, that is.

I wasn't the same woman who'd driven up to the ranch with my belongings in the back of my car. I knew now that I truly was a Steele. I looked nothing like my father—nor my mother, for that matter—but I had his spirit. I knew it, felt it on the ranch. The freedom, the open spaces, the opportunities to stretch and grow, to be whatever I wanted. It wasn't stifling or confining. That was all intangible. Just like my feelings for Boone and Jamison. The love I had for them wasn't measurable, it wasn't a *thing*. It existed, without being seen. I knew they loved me. I knew they would be there for me no matter what. To take my burdens, to even carry them for me.

I felt the weight of their rings on my finger. I was unused to the feel of them, the sight, but it was a reminder of that love. A *tangible* reminder. So was the baby most likely growing inside me.

"There you are," my mother said, coming out onto the porch, her heels clacking on the wood boards. She had on one of her power suits, as if she'd just walked out of a committee meeting and not the front door of a ranch house in Barlow, Montana. Her dark hair was perfectly groomed, her makeup subtle and understated.

Sutton followed behind, but lingered by the door. He didn't look happy, but he never really did. He was probably the perfect person to wait with my mother because he could have withstood any interrogation she may have attempted. Out of all the men on the ranch, he'd survive unscathed. Patrick and Shamus would be crying by now.

"Here I am," I replied neutrally.

I remained at the bottom of the steps. While she had a height advantage, I had no reason to get close to her. It wasn't as if we hugged. And her security men stood on either side of her. She appeared unapproachable, not superior as she wanted. She only looked that way when I let her have that edge over me. Not any longer.

"What is that ridiculous outfit you're wearing?"

She stood, hands folded in front of her, her eyes taking in every inch of me.

I didn't look down at my button-up shirt, the jean skirt and cowboy boots I loved so much.

"You've met Sutton, I'm sure," I said, not responding to her question, to her dig.

She angled her head in his direction, but didn't look behind her. "Yes."

"May I introduce you to Jamison." I lifted my hand in his direction, then toward Boone. They remained behind me a few feet. "And Boone." I didn't tell her anything more about them. The less she knew, the better, and I doubted she even cared.

"How quaint."

Just as I thought. "What is it you wish to speak about, Mother? Surely, you didn't come all this way for the scenery."

She pursed her lips, not liking my sarcasm. "You could at least invite me into your home."

"May I offer you and your security detail a beverage?"

"No, thank you. Sutton has seen to us."

I inwardly rolled my eyes.

"Mother, you pulled me away from something important with your unannounced visit. Please tell me why you are here."

Her eyes narrowed. I recognized the look. I'd seen it often enough. She was upset at my lack of interest in her presence.

"Perhaps we can have some privacy."

I sighed then. "You wish me to dismiss my friends while your security detail listens in? I think not. I have nothing to hide. The question is, do you?"

She turned on her heel and walked right past Sutton and into the house, the two security men following. Sutton remained where he was and I gave him a small smile as I walked past him. I heard Boone and Jamison's boots on the steps, knew they were right behind me.

I found my mother in the dining room, sitting at the head of the table as if this was a conference room and she was in charge. I remained standing, my hands on the high back of a chair at the other end.

The security men remained in the great room, nearby if I decided to jump across the table and harm their charge. Boone, Jamison and Sutton all came into the room, pulled out chairs and sat down. Three big cowboys, hats resting on the table before them, ready to listen.

My mother raised one plucked eyebrow, then said, "You told me you turned down the job offers you've received."

"I did."

"Why?"

"I didn't wish to live in Iceland."

She lifted her hand, gave a quick wave as if pushing Iceland to the side.

"The company in Charlotte didn't seem like a good fit," I continued.

"But the one with Borstar would be much more accommodating. You may complete your dissertation and have the job. They will be quite flexible, I'm sure, with someone of your abilities." She folded her manicured hands on the table.

I studied her closely. Remained silent. Considered her. She'd come eighteen-hundred miles for something important. Something important to *her*. She didn't care about me. And she *really* didn't care about Aiden Steele. She wanted to erase him from her life. Probably me, too, except I held some value to her. Not love. *Value.*

I could infer so much from her words. Everything, in fact. It was so obvious now. I laughed, looking at the woman who'd given birth to me. It was as if I'd needed glasses and I'd finally put them on. It was crystal clear.

"I was sent to boarding school to get out of your life."

"That is not true," she countered. "It was to give you the best education, advantages other children could never dream of having."

Of a life devoid of love, a childhood no one would want.

"Your money paid off. I'm smart enough to see what this is all about."

She remained quiet. Poised.

"You knew about the job offer was with Borstar. Now I have to wonder how I got the job, because of you or because of my brains."

She gave a negligible shrug, but her shoulders stiffened impossibly more.

"A surveyor from Borstar was here the other day. What arrangement do you have with them?"

"I don't know what you're talking about," she countered, a little too quickly. "I didn't raise you to speak to me like this."

"You didn't raise me. Chapman Academy did."

I stepped back, turned around in a circle, bit my lip. "You're on the Committee for Energy and Commerce."

"The Environment sub-committee, to be exact," Boone clarified.

All eyes shifted to him. He'd obviously checked out more than me with his online search.

"I've been in college for five years," I continued. "It took you that long to get yourself set up within the ranks in DC and Borstar helped you. How much money did they provide to your campaign?"

My mother stood abruptly, her chair scraping across the floor. "Penelope—" Her tone held censure. Anger. Yet she kept her cool. Barely.

I cut her off with a wave of my hand. "In exchange, you gave them me." I paused, analyzed. "At first, you did. But then you tossed in Steele Ranch to what, sweeten the pot? Figured out how to use your one-night stand with Aiden Steele to your advantage."

She gasped in feigned outrage.

"The surveyor was here—what, a day early?—because you told them I'd work for them. That once I was on their payroll, they'd have access to my inheritance. Prime oil and gas land."

She pursed her lips, remained silent.

"I'm not taking the job. I'm not doing the stupid dissertation."

Her eyes narrowed. "You will do as you're told."

Boone and Jamison stood to their full height, towering over both me and my mother. Perhaps that was the DNA I'd gotten from her. Short stature.

"I'm staying here, in Barlow."

She laughed then, but it was laced with sarcasm. "And do what? Can home-grown vegetables?"

I shrugged. "Maybe I'll dig for oil. I'm certainly well versed in it. But you planned for that, pushing me into that area of study. For just this moment when you needed an insider in the field."

She sputtered, then stopped. Took a deep breath. "Do you remember what I told you would happen if you didn't follow in the Vandervelk footsteps?"

I nodded, smiled. "Oh yes. You'll cut me off. Consider it done." I stuck my arm out. Pointed. "There's the door. I don't need you. I don't need your money. I certainly never had your love."

"What do you have here in this God-forsaken place?"

I glanced at Jamison and Boone. "Everything."

She followed my gaze, raked her eyes over Boone as if he'd just wrestled a nest of snakes. "You found love with a cowboy? He's at least a decade older than you." She laughed then. "What would he want with a child like you? Oh yes, he's in it—in you—for your money, for the inheritance. At least my interests are for the good of the country. My connection with Borstar will lessen the American reliance on outside energy resources."

"No, your connection with Borstar lines your pockets and ensures your political position. Nothing more. You don't give a shit about America. You don't give a shit about anything but yourself."

Her mouth fell open then. Practically to the floor. I'd never spoken back to her like that, never used foul language.

"So you'll shack up with an old cowboy. All that education for nothing. You're a waste."

Boone took a step toward my mother, but didn't touch her. I could see the anger radiating off him in waves. "I've never hit a woman, but that might change today."

Mother paled. "How dare you—"

"You don't speak to my wife that way."

"Wife?" she sputtered.

I held up my left hand, let her see the rings on my fingers. While Jamison remained quiet, I knew he was ready to toss her out the front door if I gave him the green light.

"You are an idiot! He now has half your property."

"I don't think I formally introduced myself. I'm Boone Montgomery. Of the Butte Montgomerys." When my mother didn't even blink, he continued. "Never heard of me?"

She shook her head, writing him off. I had no idea who the Butte Montgomerys were either, but I didn't really care who his family was. Based on my mother, family didn't make a person. I just wanted Boone.

"No? Then perhaps you've heard of Nathan Montgomery, Chief Judge of the United States District Court for the District of Columbia. He's my uncle. I believe he's in your neck of the woods. Then there's Jed Montgomery, but he's a little before your time. He was Senator from Montana back in 1924. Then there was his father, Garrison Montgomery, who was one of the great Copper Kings. You've heard of them. They had more money than the Rockefellers, but that was only a small amount of money. It's been over a hundred years and I'm sure the sum's much bigger now. Are those enough big names for you or did you want me to go further back on my family tree?"

Mother sniffed. "So she married you, after two weeks? She must want you for all that money."

"So am I after her money or is she after mine?" he asked. When she realized she'd gotten caught in her own words, Boone relaxed, smiled. "You think she's after me for my money? Please. She wants me for my big dick."

I choked on my own spit. Jamison outright laughed. Sutton's lips quirked up, his version of a smile.

"That will be quite enough," she replied tartly.

"That's right. We're done here."

She glanced down the table at me, but didn't say anything.

"Tell Borstar to stay off my land or I'll have them arrested. And you as well. You're not welcome here. At first, I thought you walked away from my father. My *real* father. But now, I'm sure he walked away from you. What were you guys, drunk? Is that how he got you pregnant?"

I shook my head when she pursed her lips so tight, it looked as if she were sucking on a lemon. She did flush a bright red, but made no comment. It didn't matter. I didn't really want to know about her one-night stand.

"If you come back, or make any contact with me, I'll talk," I added. "About Borstar. About Aiden Steele."

"You'll be ruined," she said. While she was full of bravado, I saw her powerful walls crumbling.

Slowly, I shook my head. "No, I won't. You will. Goodbye, Mother."

I went around the table, stood between Jamison and Boone.

She gave me one last disdainful look, then turned and left. The security detail followed. We didn't move until the SUVs started up and pulled away, their engines fading into the summer day.

"They didn't even close the front door," Sutton said. He stood, grabbed his hat and walked out, closing the door behind him.

"Are you all right, Kitten?" Jamison asked, coming over to me, putting his hands on my shoulders, leaning down so his gray eyes met mine.

I smiled. Brilliantly. My mother was gone. For good. "Fabulous."

He smiled. "That's right, you are."

"You told that woman she'd interrupted something important."

I flicked my gaze up to Boone. "That's right. She did."

"Oh, and what was that?" he asked.

Seemingly content I wasn't going to burst into tears over the confrontation, Jamison stood to his full height, crossed his arms over his chest. Waited.

"It's not Scrabble."

16

OONE

"You really have an uncle who's a judge?" Kitten asked as I worked to undo the buttons on her shirt. Again.

This time, even if the house caught fire, I wasn't stopping.

"For a scientist, you didn't do much research." I was responding, but I had no blood left in my brain to process. It had all dropped to my pants at the sight of Kitten in her bra. Jamison knelt behind her and was helping her off with her skirt, providing her balance as she stepped out of it. Jamison stood. She was before us now in the matching black lace, her cowboy boots. And our rings.

"Fuck, Kitten," Jamison said, running a hand over his mouth. "You're the hottest thing I've ever seen."

"Get naked or those panties will be ruined," I growled. I was too far gone to be tender.

I'd been cock blocked by a parent when I was a teenager. But that had been high school. My balls ached from having to take time to deal with Congresswoman Vandervelk. And now, with Kitten undoing the clasp on her bra and seeing her luscious breasts bounce free, I groaned. I knew how they felt, tasted. I watched as her little upturned nipples hardened.

Jamison glanced at me, then back to her chest. "One for each of us."

I liked the way he thought.

We moved on her then. She stepped back, once, then again until the backs of her legs bumped Jamison's bed and she dropped down so she sat on the edge of the mattress. We'd made it to his cabin—we weren't fucking her in the main house. We wanted privacy, and lots of it for what we were going to do.

Jamison dropped back to his knees and got his mouth on her, sucking a nipple hard enough his cheeks pulled in. Her hands tangled in his hair as his eyes slipped closed.

I joined him, cupping her other breast, laving the nipple. "I'm rich, Kitten," I said, before wrapping my lips around the tip, grazed my teeth over it.

"I don't care about your money."

"Are you sure?" I asked, glancing up at her, seeing her with her eyes closed, her lips parted. Her cheeks were flushed, the pink color spreading down her neck and almost to our mouths.

"I didn't even know you had it until a little while ago."

She gasped, dropped her hand on my head, curled her fingers and tugged. "I should...I should be upset, but I'm not."

We took our mouths off of her, Jamison with a loud pop. Her nipples were a cherry red, glistening from our mouths.

"Why not?" I asked.

Her eyes fluttered open and she slid her hand around to cup my jaw. She smiled, so sweet, so pure. Her pale eyes held mine. "Because I'm only interested in your big dick."

I laughed, leaned forward and kissed her. And kissed her.

"Hey!" Jamison said. "What about me and my big dick?"

I pulled back. Kitten reached out for Jamison, leaned forward and kissed him too. "Yes, you and your big dick, too. I love both your dicks equally."

"Good, because we're going to fuck you at the same time," Jamison added. He stood, began to strip. "The lube's in the drawer, Boone."

I moved to get the lube, tossed it on the bed. We'd be needing it. Lots of it. I'd claim her virgin ass, but I'd do it carefully. She loved ass play and I knew she'd love this. Kitten was so fucking passionate, so sexually responsive. She'd come, and hard.

Jamison dropped down on the bed beside Kitten, his knees bent and his feet touching the floor. His dick was hard and pointing straight up. He crooked a finger and Kitten moved over him, straddling his waist, the cowboy boots sexy as hell. Her breasts swung down, brushed his bare chest.

I loved seeing the black lace on her ass, but it had to go. Grabbing the band at the waist, I carefully tugged, tore the delicate fabric so it was in two pieces in my hands. She gasped, but said nothing as she watched it flutter to the floor.

"I warned you, Kitten."

Jamison shifted then, one hand on her hip, the other between her parted thighs, sliding in and out, testing her readiness.

From my vantage point, I couldn't miss how wet she was, the way his fingers came out of her pussy coated with her sticky honey.

"Please, Jamison. I'm ready." She shifted her hips forward so he slipped out. With one hand on his shoulder, she gripped the base of his dick and hovered over him. "I don't need to come first. I need you in me. Now."

Jamison didn't respond, most likely because she'd gotten her little fingers wrapped around him. But she'd slipped in the broad head and he groaned. He knew she was ready and wasn't going to argue. He wanted in.

So did I, but I had to wait. Her pussy might be ready for a dick, but her ass wasn't. Not yet. I grabbed the lube, flipped the lid and squirted some of it onto my fingers. I watched as Kitten fucked Jamison, took his dick nice and deep, then lifted off. Watched the way her virgin hole winked at me as I knew she clenched her pussy.

It was time. I moved toward her, slid my coated

fingers over her. It was time for her to bring us together as one. The one person who could make us a family.

Our Kitten.

JAMISON

I wasn't sure if I was going to last. Being inside Kitten, having her ride my dick, using it for her own pleasure had pre-cum coming out in little spurts. It was as if there was too much cum in my balls and I had to get some of it out. She was so fucking wet, she needed none of it to get her slick to take all of me. Nope, she slid right down in one quick slide.

The way she'd handled her mother had made my dick hard. Insane, really, but it had. She was smart, a fucking ball buster and gorgeous as hell. I was so proud of her, so insanely in love with her, I was losing my mind. And seeing our rings on her fingers was my undoing. She belonged to us. No legal document was needed. Just her words, her love. The rings a physical proof. My dick buried deep another one. And soon, Boone would join me in her. We'd prove to her she was everything, the center of our world.

I gripped one curvy hip and lush tit, cupped it, kneaded it as she moved.

The sound of the flip top on the lube made me thank every god out there. And when Boone leaned in and began to get her ass all ready for him, she stilled, leaned forward. I took that opportunity to lift my head and take a nipple back into my mouth, suck on it. Hard. Hard enough that it made her walls rhythmically pulse around me.

Sweat beaded my brow. She barely moved, just circled her hips. I was going to die. Killed not from Kitten's claws, but by her sweet pussy.

She groaned, her eyes widening as she relaxed her neck, her head dropping and her silky hair falling in a curtain around us. I knew Boone was working her, carefully opening her up with more than just a finger. Two, possibly even three.

"You're going to come, Kitten, just from this. From Boone opening that ass up and you riding my dick. And while you're coming, Boone's going to fill you right up. You'll have both of us, nice and deep."

I kept my words low, even. Crooning promises. I dropped both my hands to her hips as I widened my knees, parted her for Boone.

I took over, lifting and lowering her as I rocked my hips up, fucking her in shallow strokes, getting Boone's fingers to go even deeper. I could feel him through the thin membrane that separated us.

Kitten's eyes fell closed and her whole body softened, giving herself over to us. I met Boone's gaze over her shoulder. He was barely hanging on. He gave a nod and I thrust a little deeper, grit my teeth at the exquisite feel of it. The feel of her. "So beautiful, that's it. Come."

 ENNY

I WAS MINDLESS. Boneless. I felt their hands, their dicks, the bliss. I heard their words, their praise. But I was lost to the pleasure. I'd come riding one of them before. Several times. But as I came all over Jamison, Boone had pressed into my bottom, the broad head stretching me wide, wider, even wider still until it silently popped in. That stretch, the burn of it only added to the orgasm and it just went on and on.

I was so full, completely surrounded by them. I dropped onto Jamison's chest; my arms couldn't hold me up any longer. I panted into the crook of his neck, breathed in his manly scent, tasted the salt of his sweat. His chest hair tickled my sensitive breasts as lower...lower they ruled me.

My pussy was rippling and milking Jamison's dick as Boone pressed in, pulled back, the nerve endings that I hadn't even known I had flared to life.

"Look at you take us both. Such a good girl," Boone murmured. I felt his fingertips slide down my back as he rocked into me a little more. I was slick, so slick from all the lube. I felt a trickle of it now and then as he added more, ensuring I could take all of him.

Jamison shifted his hips, thrust up and I moaned. He hadn't come. Only stilled as I recovered.

"We're not done, Kitten," he breathed as he kissed my hair.

I groaned, squeezed them both.

Boone gave my bottom a little swat. "She knows how to make us come."

I grinned, kissed Jamison's neck. His words revived me, made me feel powerful.

Both their cocks were in me. I felt the press of Boone's hips against my bottom and I knew he was all the way in.

It was *almost* too much. Jamison's hands came to my arms and he pushed me up, held me there so I was wedged between them and completely at their mercy.

"Ready, Kitten?"

I nodded, clenched down.

They moved then, alternating their in-and-out motions. I groaned, low and deep. "God, it's so good. Too much. Not enough. I need...oh, I'm going to come!"

All kinds of words came out of my mouth. I couldn't think, couldn't understand how I was feeling. It was so intense, tears came to my eyes, my ears tingled. I was completely theirs. My body didn't belong to me in this moment. I had no control, nothing to do except give myself to them. Both of them.

"Come, Kitten. Just let go. We're here. We'll catch you, keep you safe. Always."

Boone leaned forward and I felt the press of him along my back, felt his lips at my neck. "Mine."

"Mine," Jamison repeated.

They stopped talking then, the only sounds filling the room were of our raw fucking. Slippery and wet, flesh pounding flesh, slick skin sliding, touching.

I came on a scream, my body tensing as they continued to take me, to push me through it with their dicks until Jamison stiffened, groaned, filled me with hot pulses of cum.

The only signal of Boone's release was his fingers digging into my hips. He held himself still, buried deep. His groans mixed with our ragged breathing.

I was spent. Ruined for anything but them. Nothing would ever compare.

Jamison's arms dropped to the mattress, Boone planted a hand beside my hip to hold himself up.

I had no idea how long we remained that way, but Boone finally pulled out, slowly and carefully. I winced at the burn, felt the flood of cum that seeped from me. I lifted my head and took him in. He hadn't taken off his clothes, only opened his pants until his cock was free and they fell about his thighs.

Jamison lifted me off him, another torrent of cum slipping from me as he placed me beside him on the bed, snuggled against his side.

The water came on in the shower and Boone returned, stroked a hand down my thigh.

"I love you, Kitten."

I rolled to my back and he leaned over me, kissed me tenderly. I reached up, stroked his face. "I love you, too."

He grabbed my wrist, turned it over and kissed the rings they'd put on my fingers. His dark eyes met mine, held. I saw the heat, the fire. The love.

"Hey, what about me?" Jamison asked playfully and I rolled my eyes.

Boone lifted his head and I turned mine, kissed Jamison too.

"Was that okay?" Jamison asked, his lips roving over my face.

"Too good."

"Sore?"

I clenched. "A little."

I'd just taken two guys at once. Not long ago I'd been a virgin. I'd come a long way. My pussy, my ass and my heart.

"We'll get you all cleaned up and then a bag of frozen peas, if you need it. Then we'll do it again."

I reached up, tugged Boone so he sat beside me. Jamison on the other side. This was where I wanted to be. With them. Here. Wherever here was. It didn't matter. I was home.

I lifted my hands, cupped both of their faces, felt the scruff on their jaws. *Mine.*

"Promises, promises."

NOTE FROM VANESSA

Don't worry, there's more Steele Ranch to come!

But guess what? I've got some bonus content for you. Find out which long-lost daughter arrives next...and a little bit of extra lovin' for Penny from Jamison and Boone. So sign up for my mailing list. There will be special bonus content for each Steele Ranch book, just for my subscribers. Signing up will let you hear about my next release as soon as it is out, too (and you get a free book...wow!)

As always...thanks for loving my books and the wild ride!

Vanessa

WANT MORE?

The Steele Ranch series continues with Tangled! Read chapter I now!

TANGLED - CHAPTER ONE

CRICKET

"You've got ten minutes," Schmidt growled, pushing an outfit at me. "Put this on and come back out. Find some shoes that fit." He pointed to the floor behind me. The thump of the base from the song blaring in the main room came through the floor, the thin walls. The scent of stale beer and smoke lingered.

I glanced about at my new reality. The space was small, an oversized closet. A fluorescent light bar affixed to the ceiling cast everything in a harsh glare. Two moveable hanging racks flanked me, lingerie and the skimpiest of outfits hanging from them. Red lace, shiny metal lamé, cheerleader and schoolgirl skirts along with midriff baring tops. On the floor were a variety of fuck-me shoes with at least four-inch heels in all colors of patent pleather.

I glanced down to what he'd shoved in my hands. A nurse's outfit. A white dress—if it could be called that, with short sleeves and even shorter hem—with Velcro closures on the front instead of buttons. Beneath it, I was to wear a white bikini top, made up of two tiny triangles, and a matching G-string, also white, which had a red plus sign right on the front as if my crotch was the source of medical help.

My stomach roiled at the thought of what they expected. I couldn't go out there and strip! I couldn't even put the outfit on.

"I can't do this," I said, pleading. One last time. I'd been doing it for the past two hours, ever since they'd taken me from my apartment.

"You don't have a choice, sweetheart." Schmidt—I assumed it was his last name, but it was all I knew him by —was in his fifties, built like a whiskey barrel, and had a cigarette dangling from his lip. I'd seen the gun in the waistband of his pants. Nothing unusual since it was Montana and everyone carried, even little old ladies, but I didn't think his was as much for protection as enforcement of his wishes.

While he hadn't laid a finger on me, I knew he wouldn't hesitate to do so if he wanted. Same for his sidekick, Rocky. Especially after Rocky had grabbed me and dragged me out of my apartment and to my car. I'd had no choice but to drive us to this seedy place on the edge of town. I'd had thoughts of jumping out at a stoplight, but I knew he'd just drag me back, pissed off.

Maybe it would've been better to have jumped into an intersection instead of being where I was now. I couldn't get past Schmidt since he was almost as wide as the doorway, but even if I could, Rocky was looming behind him. And with both of them armed, I didn't risk it. I didn't think they were killers, but I didn't put rape past them. Their way to persuade me most likely involved me on my knees or on my back.

"I paid you the amount I owed," I reminded him. Again. Desperation laced my words.

He laughed at that, his eyes roaming over me in my jeans and plain t-shirt. "Not the interest."

"I paid that, too. Twenty percent."

He grinned, slowly shook his head as if he were talking to an idiot. Maybe I was one since I was standing in the back room of a seedy strip club. "Sweetheart, I told you, it's compound interest. Didn't you learn anything about that in the fancy college classes you borrowed money to take?"

The anatomy and physiology class I'd taken covered how his ACL would be torn if I kicked him in the knee the way I wanted, but it hadn't had any quizzes on being screwed over by a shifty loan shark. I'd been so stupid taking money from him. I could practically see the diploma I'd worked so hard to get, except a new transmission had put me behind, no matter how many extra shifts I'd worked.

He grinned, his crooked teeth yellow. He had me, and I had a very good feeling the compound interest would never go away. I was fucked. So damned fucked.

"That outfit's special, just for you since you're studying to be a nurse and all."

I was nauseated, realizing he remembered why I'd

borrowed money from him in the first place. It hadn't been to pay for a drug habit, dammit! It was college, to fucking better myself! How long had he been keeping an eye on me?

"I don't know how to strip," I said, licking my dry lips, stating the obvious. I could barely dance; my friends always teased me that I had no rhythm.

"You take your clothes off every damned day," he countered. "It's not that hard, and as long as you show those big tits and tease the guys with a glimpse of a tight pussy at the end, no one will know."

Tears burned at the back of my eyes. "I've never done this before."

"Sweetheart, you're the Virgin Nurse. Everyone's going to love watching you get your stripper cherry popped out there. You only have to strip until your debt's paid."

"Two thousand dollars?" I replied. "That's one-hundred percent interest and a hell of a lot of stripping."

He lifted a beefy shoulder. "You can take customers in the back room. Lap dances pay more, especially if you give them a happy ending."

Gag. I knew what he meant. Fucking strangers or sucking their dicks for extra money. A happy ending for me would be to walk out of here and never see him again.

"You can show me how good you are after closing." He winked and I threw up a little in my mouth.

I wasn't a virgin and I liked sex a little wild, but there was no way I was doing anything with him, or anyone else in this place. I slowly shook my head, my eyes wide.

"I can go to the police," I added, although the threat, I knew, was empty.

His smile shifted to lethal. "Tell anyone and sucking dicks for a twenty isn't all you'll be doing. Hope you liked that semester of school. Payback's a bitch." He just smiled. "Ten minutes."

He stepped back, slammed the door shut, making the metal hangers rattle.

I gulped, let the tears fall. Shit, *shit!* I couldn't do this. I couldn't stand before a roomful of strange men and dance, let alone take my clothes off. I'd been naked in front of guys before, but those times had been completely different. Consensual. Fun. A little wild. No, a whole lot wild. But this?

I had money. *Now.* Not at the beginning of summer semester when I'd borrowed from Schmidt. Last week when I'd received the official letter in the mail, I hadn't believed it. My father, whom I'd never known, had died and left me money. Lots of it. But if I told Schmidt about the inheritance, he'd want more than the two grand. He'd never leave me alone and that was why I kept it a secret. I wanted to tell him, desperately, so I could get out of here, but at this point, I doubted he'd even believe me.

I'm the heiress to the Steele fortune.

Yeah, right. He'd seen my apartment, my older car. Hell, I'd borrowed money from him. No millionaire needed to borrow money from a loan shark.

The door opened and I jumped, the G-string sliding off the hanger and falling to the floor. "You're not changing."

Rocky. Schmidt was definitely in charge and he was

all business. I didn't doubt he fucked the women who worked at his club, but he wasn't like Rocky. Rocky was all sick leer. Handsy. He'd take me right now if he could get away with it. And he scared me more than the boss.

He bent down, picked up the G-string so it dangled from one of his fingers. "I can help." His slick grin made my stomach roil.

"I'm going to be sick." I put a hand over my mouth. Perhaps it was the look on my face or the way I probably turned a funky shade of green, but he jumped back and pointed to the door across the hall. I bolted for the ladies' room and into the back stall, leaned over the toilet and dry heaved.

The song switched and I knew my turn was coming closer. With one hand on the stained white wall, I caught my breath.

Finished, my stomach hurting, I stood, realizing I still held the hanger with the nurse's outfit. No way in hell could I put that on.

"Five minutes," Rocky shouted, pounding on the door. He might have wanted to help me get into the sexy nurse's outfit, but it seemed he drew the line at holding my hair back as I threw up. He'd remained in the hall. For that, I was grateful.

I had to get out of here, out of this. I'd borrowed the money, yes. I knew, going in, that it was probably stupid, but I'd paid Schmidt back in full. On time. Worked overtime to do so. I never did drugs in my life, didn't even drink. Had never smoked a cigarette. I'd seen too much in my time in foster care to know what all that did to people and quickly learned no one else was going to take care of me. All my money went to my bills and to school, so I could get my nursing degree and get out of the paycheck-to-paycheck existence.

But Schmidt just wanted to fuck with me, to drag me down. To make extra cash off the backs of those who unfortunately got involved with him. I'd paid him back. I was tired of being taken advantage of. I wasn't having it, not again.

I stepped out of the stall, looked around. Dingy mint green tile, a cracked mirror. Not enough women came to the strip club to warrant a remodel. But unlike the closet, there was a window. A small one, but a way out. I went to it, fiddled with the latch, then glanced over my shoulder. Rocky could come in at any time. He would, I knew, in less than five minutes if I didn't come out.

I flipped the worn lock, put my palms on the middle part of the frame and pushed. It shifted, but the paint was old, the wood swollen, my efforts producing a loud creak of protest. Glancing over my shoulder once again, I wondered if Rocky had heard it. Hopefully, the heavy beat of the music hid the noise. A draft of cool air hit me from the small opening I'd created, spurring me to get the thing open. Two inches of freedom and my adrenaline surged. The window was small, but if I could get it open, I could squeeze out. I would, no matter what. I pushed and worked it open, more, then more still until I could fit through.

I shimmied, squeezed, pushed and worked myself through the opening, putting my hands out to block my head as I fell the few feet to the pavement. Looking around, I got my bearings. I was in the parking lot, the dumpster in front of me, meaning I was on the far side, away from the entrance. It wasn't dark yet, maybe seven o'clock or so. While the lot was partially full, no one was around. No one witnessed my escape. I just had to hope the place was too low-class for security cameras, at least on this side of the building.

I stood, wiped my hands on my jeans to get the grit off, then ran toward my car. I still had my leather purse slung crosswise over my body. With fumbling fingers, I grabbed my keys from within, looked back to make sure Rocky hadn't found me missing yet. I only had a minute or two at the most.

Once in my car, I prayed that it would start. They didn't see me much as a threat, knowing that they could intimidate me—or hurt me—if I didn't keep coming back night after night and strip until the damned debt was paid. They didn't need to hold me hostage to keep me a prisoner.

No fucking way. I wasn't coming back. Ever. I had to get out of here. Out of this parking lot, out of town. I started my POS car and sped out of the lot, barely slowing to make the turn onto the street. My heart jumped in my throat as I saw in the rearview mirror Rocky's head sticking out the open bathroom window, his eyes murderous.

I couldn't go home, not even for clothes or the money I had hidden. They knew where I lived and no doubt that would be the first place they'd look for me. All they'd do was grab me and bring me back, the next time with a little more anger and aggression. Probably have a little *fun* with me first. They'd underestimated me tonight, thankfully, but I knew they wouldn't a second time.

I put my foot to the floor at the far side of town, the buildings receding behind me. I needed to get lost. Hide. I knew just where to go.

Keep reading Tangled now!

ABOUT THE AUTHOR

Vanessa Vale is the *USA Today* Bestselling author of over 40 books, sexy romance novels, including her popular Bridgewater historical romance series and hot contemporary romances featuring unapologetic bad boys who don't just fall in love, they fall hard. When she's not writing, Vanessa savors the insanity of raising two boys, is figuring out how many meals she can make with a pressure cooker, and teaches a pretty mean karate class. While she's not as skilled at social media as her kids, she loves to interact with readers.

www.vanessavaleauthor.com

ALSO BY VANESSA VALE

Steele Ranch

Spurred

Wrangled

Tangled

Hitched

Lassoed

Bridgewater County Series

Ride Me Dirty

Claim Me Hard

Take Me Fast

Hold Me Close

Make Me Yours

Kiss Me Crazy

Mail Order Bride of Slate Springs Series

A Wanton Woman

A Wild Woman

A Wicked Woman

Bridgewater Ménage Series

Their Runaway Bride

Their Kidnapped Bride

Their Wayward Bride

Their Captivated Bride

Their Treasured Bride

Their Christmas Bride

Their Reluctant Bride

Their Stolen Bride

Their Brazen Bride

Their Bridgewater Brides- Books 1-3 Boxed Set

Outlaw Brides Series

Flirting With The Law

MMA Fighter Romance Series

Fight For Her

Wildflower Bride Series

Rose

Hyacinth

Dahlia

Daisy

Lily

Montana Men Series

The Lawman

The Cowboy

The Outlaw

Standalone Reads

Twice As Delicious

Western Widows

Sweet Justice

CPSIA information can be obtained
at www.ICGtesting.com
Printed in the USA
LVHW041048171219
640672LV00005B/172/P